AMBUSHED!

Suddenly the door to the room burst open.

Clint reacted immediately. He pushed the stunned girl beside him away with his left hand and with his right grabbed the gun holster hanging on the bedpost. There was a muzzle flash from the door, then the sound of two shots, one Clint's, and the other someone else's. The man in the door grunted, staggered, dropped his gun and slid to the floor.

DON'T MISS THESE
ALL-ACTION WESTERN SERIES
FROM THE BERKLEY PUBLISHING GROUP

THE GUNSMITH by J. R. Roberts
Clint Adams was a legend among lawmen, outlaws, and ladies. They called him . . . the Gunsmith.

LONGARM by Tabor Evans
The popular long-running series about U.S. Deputy Marshal Long—his life, his loves, his fight for justice.

SLOCUM by Jake Logan
Today's longest-running action Western. John Slocum rides a deadly trail of hot blood and cold steel.

BUSHWHACKERS by B. J. Lanagan
An action-packed series by the creators of Longarm! The rousing adventures of the most brutal gang of cutthroats ever assembled—Quantrill's Raiders.

THE GUNSMITH

196

THE COUNTERFEIT CLERGYMAN

J. R. ROBERTS

JOVE BOOKS, NEW YORK

THE COUNTERFEIT CLERGYMAN

A Jove Book / published by arrangement with
the author

PRINTING HISTORY
Jove edition / May 1998

The Penguin Putnam Inc. World Wide Web site address is
http://www.penguinputnam.com

ISBN: 0-515-12279-3

A JOVE BOOK®
Jove Books are published by The Berkley Publishing Group,
a member of Penguin Putnam Inc.,
200 Madison Avenue, New York, New York 10016.
JOVE and the "J" design are trademarks
belonging to Jove Publications, Inc.

PRINTED IN THE UNITED STATES OF AMERICA

10 9 8 7 6 5 4 3 2 1

THE GUNSMITH

196

THE COUNTERFEIT CLERGYMAN

PROLOGUE

Frank Hastings looked at the girl lying next to him in bed. Her name was Carmen, she was nineteen, and she had come to his bed very willingly. Although she was young, she had a woman's body. Large, firm breasts, meaty thighs and buttocks, rounded shoulders and upper arms. She had lots of black hair that fanned out around her head as she slept. She was lying on her belly, the sheet down around her ankles. He put his hand on her buttocks and rubbed them softly, causing her to moan but not to awaken.

He got to his knees next to her and slid his hand down between her thighs. Gently, he probed her, and she spread her legs to allow him access to her. He rubbed his left hand over her buttocks again, while probing with his right. He felt the hair between her legs grow moist, and then his finger was sliding along her moistened slit. She moaned and pressed herself into his touch as he slid his finger inside of her, and he smiled, knowing that she was definitely awake now.

He straddled her from behind and slid his thick, hard penis between her thighs. When the spongy head of his shaft found her wetness, he slid into her easily and she gasped and took the bedsheet in both hands.

As he started to move in her, she got to her hands and knees, the better for her to press back against him as he thrust himself into her. She did so with great pleasure, because this was what God wanted her to do.

"Aieee, Dios mío," she moaned in Spanish as he gripped her hips and began to move in and out of her harder and faster.

Hastings ran one hand over her back, down over her buttocks, enjoying the smooth, silky feel of her skin. It was already warm, and her body began to become slick with sweat. He put both hands on her hips again and pulled her to him as he thrust into her again and again. She looked back at him over her shoulder, and the look on her face was one of pure animal pleasure. It inflamed him even more and suddenly he felt as if he would burst.

He exploded inside of her, filling her with what felt to her like a million tiny needles, all giving pleasure to her as they invaded her body.

At nineteen Carmen had been very inexperienced when she first came to Hastings's bed. She had learned much over the past few months, and made up in enthusiasm what she might have lacked in experience.

At forty-eight Hastings sometimes felt like a dirty old man when he took Carmen to bed, but that was not the case this morning. This morning, as he continued to empty himself inside of her, he felt like a bull, twenty years younger than his years.

"Jesus," he said, collapsing next to her on the bed.

"You should not say that," she said.

"What?"

"The Lord's name."

He smiled at her.

"I know, Carmen." He touched her face, stroked her hair. "I'm sorry, but you have a way of making me forget who I am supposed to be."

"You say such pretty things." She smiled back, revealing strong, white teeth behind a dazzlingly beautiful smile. She came into his arms then and they slept.

When she woke he was sitting up in bed, writing something on a piece of paper.

"What are you writing?" she asked.

He looked at her and folded the paper.

"Nothing."

"A poem?"

He hesitated, then nodded.

"Another poem?"

"Yes."

"You are always writing poems."

He smiled at her and said, "I have always written poetry."

"When will you let me read some?" she asked.

"Someday," he said, "maybe someday."

Before she could say anything else there was a knock at the door.

"Padre?" a voice called.

"Yes?" Hastings replied.

"*Por favor*, we need you, Padre," a man said.

"Is it important?" Hastings asked.

"*Sí*, Padre," the man said, "it is *muy importante*."

Hastings looked at Carmen, and she smiled and said, "You must go."

"We're not finished," he said.

"I will be here," she said, and rolled onto her back, revealing her firm, round breasts and brown nipples.

He started to reach for her when the knock was repeated on the door.

"I'm coming, Paulo," he said, quitting the bed. "That is you, isn't it, Paulo?"

There was a pause, and then the man said, "*Sí*, Padre, it is me."

"Wait for me by the front door, Paulo."

"*Sí*," Paulo said, and Hastings heard him walk away.

He grabbed his clothes from the floor and slipped into them. For a moment he stared at the trunk in the corner where the gun belt was, but he decided to leave it there. After all, it had been in there for three months. But it had also been calling to him during that time. Sometimes, at night, when he was in bed with Carmen fast asleep next to him, he thought he could hear the gun inside the trunk.

"Frank?" Carmen said.

"Hmmm?"

"You must go," she said from the bed, startling him from his reverie.

"Yes," he said, "I know, Carmen."

He started for the door.

"Father Frank?" she said.

"Yes?"

She got to her knees on the bed, flaunting her nakedness, and touched her neck.

"Your collar."

"Oh," he said, "yes."

He couldn't very well be "Father Frank" without his clerical collar, could he? He took it from the dresser top, put it on, and went out the door to see why the people needed him this time.

If he'd known it was going to be this hard to be a priest he might not have taken the job on.

Valhalla was right on the border between Texas and Mexico. Like El Paso it straddled both sides, but unlike El Paso it was not a very large town on either side of the border.

Hastings lived on the Mexican side and rarely crossed over. The people on the Mexican side often came to him for help and advice. The people on the American side had no priest, so they sometimes crossed the border to see him.

Today, the people who wanted to see him were from the American side of the border.

They wanted to get married.

ONE

Valhalla reminded Clint of his time in El Paso, with Dallas Stoudemire, before the lawman was killed. He had stood by Stoudemire for a while, but he could not stay in El Paso forever. With lesser men to watch his back, the lawman was eventually shot and killed. Clint felt badly about it, and didn't like being reminded of it. Therefore, he meant for his stay in Valhalla to be a short one.

Clint knew what Valhalla meant. It was an old name for the home of the gods. This Valhalla, however, didn't look like it had even one god.

Clint was on his way to Mexico, and had taken this route only because he had never taken it before. He had heard of Valhalla but had never been there. Now that he was riding down the main street he wondered who had chosen the name. It must have been an American who named it. Did the Mexicans even know about the Norse gods? Clint only knew about them because he'd read about them once. The possibility that there were many gods instead of just one had fascinated him at one time. A god of War, a god of Thunder, a god of the Underworld, a goddess of Love. What god, though, would come to this dirty, dusty place?

As he rode past the saloon he saw the name written

5

above it: The Asgard Saloon. If he remembered correctly, Asgard was the highest world of the gods, sort of like Heaven. Somebody had named a *saloon* after it!

He rode until he came to the livery. He left Duke in the capable if somewhat scarred hands of a liveryman named Juan and carried his rifle and saddlebags away. As he left the livery he looked to his left and saw the wooden bridge which spanned the river, which narrowed nicely at that point to join the two sides of the same town.

He had asked Juan where the nearest hotel was and received directions. As he approached it he wondered what name would be above the door this time. He was not disappointed. The hotel was called The Midgard, which was the second level, the middle world, of Norse legends.

He entered the hotel and saw that the lobby furnishings went with the name. There were paintings on the walls of many of the Norse gods. He wondered if any of them were worth money. He knew a little about Norse legends from reading, but he knew nothing of art.

The lobby was nicely furnished, and the Midgard seemed somewhat ostentatious for a town like Valhalla. He wondered if there had been big plans for the town which might have gone wrong.

"Can I help you, sir?" the clerk asked. He was in his twenties, tall and well-dressed, and well-schooled in his job. He was pleasant and gave Clint the impression that he was delighted that he was there.

"This is quite a hotel you have here," Clint said.

"Thank you, sir. A room?"

"Yes."

The clerk got a key and turned the register around so Clint could sign in.

"Mr. . . . Adams," the clerk said, reading the name. He gave no indication that he might have recognized it. "How long will you be staying?"

"A day," Clint said, "maybe two." Valhalla was becoming more interesting by the moment. He thought he might stay an extra day, just to investigate its origins some.

"Are you aware of the significance of the town's name? And the name of the hotel?"

"And the saloon," Clint said. "Yes, I'm aware of the myths of the Norse gods."

"Excellent," the man said. "Not many people are, you know."

"I wonder if you might tell me whose idea all of this was."

"Well, that's easy," the clerk said. "Mr. Odin owns the hotel and the saloon, and it was he who named the town."

"Odin?"

"Yes," the clerk said, "Odin was the King of the—"

"I know who Odin was," Clint said. "This fella's name is really Odin?"

"Well," the clerk said, "just between you and me? His name is really O'Deen"—the clerk spelled it—"but he likes to say Odin. You didn't hear it from me, hmm?"

"My lips are sealed," Clint said.

The clerk, who seemed somewhat effete when you spoke to him for this long, handed Clint a key and said, "Enjoy your stay."

"I'm sure I'll find it very interesting," Clint said, accepting the key.

TWO

Clint left his gear in his room and went out to take a look at Valhalla in all its glory. There wasn't much glory to see, though. Except for the hotel and the saloon, the remainder of the town seemed somewhat run-down. Toward the river it even fell into a state of disrepair. Clint wondered how the Mexican side looked, but decided to save that for later. It was hot, and walking had built up a thirst. He decided to check out the inside of the Asgard Saloon.

When he entered the saloon he was surprised to see a huge, red-haired, red-bearded man behind the bar. If he remembered correctly—and so far he thought he had—Odin was supposed to be huge, with a mass of red hair and a red beard.

Clint looked around the saloon, which was less than half full at a time of day when saloons in most towns would be filling up.

"Can I help you, friend?" the red-bearded bartender asked.

"Are you . . . Odin?" Clint decided to take a guess.

"Ha!" The man laughed loudly. "An educated man. Welcome to Valhalla, sir, and welcome to Asgard. I am indeed Odin—Jack Odin, if you will."

The huge bartender stuck out his hand and Clint shook it. The man probably stood six eight, and his hand dwarfed Clint's.

"You have a beer coming on the house, sir . . . if beer is what you want?"

"It is."

"Coming up, then."

Clint waited while Odin drew him a beer and came back with it. He looked around the saloon, and if he hadn't already known that Odin owned it and the hotel he would have guessed, at least, that the same man had decorated it. Over the bar was a huge painting of one of the Norse goddesses. His best guess would be that it was the goddess of Love, because she was naked.

"I see you're admiring Freyja."

"Oh, yes," Clint said, "that's who it is. The goddess of Love, isn't she?"

"Freyja was associated with love and war in Norse legend," Odin said. "Are you a student of the Norse legend, sir?"

"My name is Clint Adams," Clint said to Odin, "but you can call me Clint."

"Adams," Odin repeated. "I know the name. It's a pleasure to have you in my shop. You can call me Jack."

"Well, Jack, I don't pretend to be a student of Norse myth—"

"Legend," Jack Odin corrected him. "Around here we call them legends, not myths."

"I stand corrected," Clint said, "and I apologize."

"That's all right. You were saying?"

"I did some reading on the . . . legends once, that's all."

"And you remember them?"

"Some," Clint said. "I remembered enough to know the names Valhalla, Asgard, and Midgard."

"Ah, are you staying in my hotel?"

"I am. Is there another in town?"

"There is," Odin said, "but we don't really speak of it."

"I'll remember."

"Do you know that painting?" Odin asked, pointing across the room.

Directly opposite the painting of the naked Freyja was a painting of three women who were anything but naked. No less beautiful than Freyja—or slightly less so—they wore armor that covered their torsos but could not hide the thrust of their breasts.

"The Valkyries, right?"

"By the gods, sir," Odin said, slapping him on the back so hard he almost spilled his beer, "it's a pleasure to talk with a knowledgeable man. They are, indeed, the Valkyries. Clint, you've earned yourself another beer on the house."

"I'll take you up on that, Jack," Clint said, "as soon as I finish this one."

"Take your time," Odin said. "We can talk some more while you drink it."

Clint took a dutiful swallow and then gestured with the mug.

"Are you always this, uh, busy?"

"We get busier," Odin said. "In a couple of hours the girls will get here. The men usually come in to see them."

"Valkyries?"

The man shook his head and said, "Saloon girls."

"Ah."

"But they're pretty ones," Odin said, "pretty enough for Odin himself."

"You?"

"No," the man said, "I meant the real Odin."

"Oh."

Clint finished his beer and accepted the second one from Jack Odin.

"So how long will you be staying in town?" the saloon/hotel owner asked.

"A day, maybe two," Clint said.

"On your way to where?"

"Mexico."

"Anywhere in particular?"

"I want to see some water," Clint said, "and maybe visit an old friend."

"Well, we're happy to have you here even for a day or two."

"Jack," Clint said, leaning on the bar, "since we're talking . . ."

"Yes?"

"Can I ask you something, frankly?"

"I prefer frank talk when I can get it, Clint," Odin said, "but let me see if I can guess. You want to know why I haven't opened my saloon and hotel in a better place, right? A more lively town?"

"Well . . . yes, that was my question."

"Well," Odin said, "there was a time when this was a livelier town, and it may be again. When I came here I had a vision, a vision of Valhalla the way I wanted it to be."

"It wasn't called Valhalla when you got here?"

"Oh, no," Odin said, "it had some awful name I don't even want to remember. I named it Valhalla."

"The townspeople let you change the name of their town?"

"Why not?" he asked. "I was opening a saloon, a hotel, I was bringing some money into town. Besides, they weren't so attached to the old name. So I suggested Valhalla at a town meeting—naturally I had to explain to them what it meant—and the rest is history—of course, it's not as successful a history as I'd like, but I've got time. Hey," he said, spreading his arms, "I'm Odin. I've got all the time in the world, eh?"

THREE

Clint remained in the Asgard long enough to find out that Odin had been right about his girls. There were three of them. They arrived separately—though minutes apart—and each planted a kiss on Odin's cheek as if he were their father.

Odin introduced each girl in turn to Clint.

The first was Roskva.

The second was Beyla.

The third was Sif.

These were names given them by Jack Odin.

Roskva was a servant of Thor. This Roskva was a very pretty, dark-haired girl with fair skin. She was slender, and small, and had a shy smile—though Clint didn't see how she could be shy and work in a saloon.

Beyla, in the legends, was a servant of the god Freyr, who was the son of Nord . . . and Clint lost track there of everything but the smell of Beyla's blond hair. She was tall, full-bodied, wearing a dress that revealed cleavage that took his breath away, and she looked Clint boldly in the eye, which he liked.

Sif was the wife of Thor, but this Sif didn't look like anyone's wife. She was red-haired and exuded sex. Slender, but taller than Roskva, her scent seemed to fill the room and men turned their heads when she entered. She was the most obviously sexual of the three women, though if Clint had a chance to choose he most certainly would have chosen Beyla.

He wondered if he'd ever get the chance to ask these three women their real names.

"What do you think?" Odin asked when the girls went to work the floor. Already the place was twice as filled as it had been when Clint entered, so Odin obviously knew his clientele.

"They're all lovely."

"You prefer Beyla, don't you?"

Clint looked at Odin, who laughed.

"I can tell," the big man said, "the way you looked at her, the way she looked at you . . . I can tell."

"That's ridiculous."

"You can have her, you know."

"I don't pay—"

"Who said anything about paying?" Odin asked, cutting him off. "All you have to do is ask her."

Clint looked at Beyla, talking to a table full of cowboys, and then back at Odin.

"She'll do it," Odin said. "She wants you, man."

"You'll tell her to do it," Clint said. "That would be the same as paying—"

"I swear," Odin said, cutting him off again and raising his hand to God—or to the gods, "I won't say a word." He dropped his hand. "Hey, a man needs some companionship."

"Well," Clint said, "we'll see."

"Hey, you're a poker player, right?"

"I've been known to play."

"A game or two usually breaks out when there are these many men in here," Odin said. "How about another beer?"

"Only if you let me pay for one."

Odin smiled, his teeth impossibly white behind his bushy red beard.

"You got a deal."

Clint nursed the third beer and continued to talk with Odin.

"What about the beard?" he asked. "And the hair?"

"The hair is mine," Odin said, grabbing a handful and tugging. "When I first became interested in the Norse gods I read all I could about Odin. When I realized he was a big man with red hair, I laughed. I grew the beard as a joke, but I liked the way it looked. I still like it. I really look like Odin, don't I?" The man asked the question with unrestrained glee.

"Yes, you do, but," Clint said warily, "you know you're not, right?"

"Of course I know that," Jack Odin said with a grin. "Of course."

FOUR

Frank Hastings was sitting at his writing table. Actually, it was simply a wooden table with wobbly legs, but he used it to write on. His room behind the church was very simple. There was a bed, large enough for him and Carmen to share, the table, and an equally rickety chair which he lowered himself into gingerly each time. There was a dresser with three drawers and the fourth missing, where he kept his meager wardrobe.

And in the corner was the trunk, where he kept the items he wanted out of sight. He also kept his writing tablets in there, most of which were filled with his poetry. Some of the tablets were blank, but he would soon have more. They were coming tonight.

He also kept bottles of whiskey in there, and he was down to his last one. It was late, and he was working on a new poem while he waited for the delivery of more whiskey and tablets.

He obtained his whiskey and tablets from the American side of town. They were available to him on the Mexican side, but he did not want anyone to know he was getting them.

Suddenly, there was a knock on his back door. The back door led outside, while the front door of his room led to a hallway and then to the church. He got up from the table and opened the back door.

"Lester," he said, "come in."

Lester was the man he paid to bring him the items he needed from the American side of Valhalla. Actually, the Mexicans did not refer to their side of the town by that name. They called it Santa Maria. They were religious, and resented that the American, Jack O'Deen, had named the town after a false religion.

"I got your stuff, uh, Father," Lester said as Hastings closed the door, "and some news."

"And no one saw you?"

"No one ever does."

Carmen was not with him tonight. When he knew Lester was coming he kept her away. She did not question when he told her to stay away. She never questioned him.

Lester gave Hastings three bottles of whiskey from one saddlebag and a half a dozen writing tablets from another. He also produced the makings for cigarettes, tobacco and paper, a half a dozen cigars, matches, and several newspapers, none of which was less than a week old.

"Thank you, Lester."

He put the items in the chest, then took some money from the table and handed it to the man. He never let Lester see that he took the money from the chest. These were the only purchases that Hastings made, and they were usually twice a month, so there was still plenty of money in the chest.

Lester counted the money and while he did so Hastings looked at him. If anything, the man seemed to have become even thinner. He did not look as if he could stand up to a stiff wind. He was probably in his twenties, but he looked older. Hastings suspected that the man was sick with some disease. He didn't cough or anything, but his pallor seemed grayer each time, his eyes more sunken.

"Thank you, Father," he said, tucking the money into his pocket.

"Now, what's this news?"

"A stranger rode into town today," Lester said. "He's staying at the hotel, the Mi—Mid—"

"Midgard?"

"Yeah," Lester said, and laughed nervously. It made him nervous to be in a church, even if he wasn't really *in* the church. "I can't say that."

"And who is he?"

"I went in and checked the register," Lester said. "It was Clint Adams."

Hastings didn't react.

"The Gunsmith."

"I know who Clint Adams is, Lester," Hastings said.

"Is it important that he's here?"

"I don't know."

"Do you want him, uh, killed?"

"Of course not. Besides, you'd probably be killed instead."

"Oh, I wouldn't do it myself," Lester said.

"Never mind," Hastings said, "it's not going to be done."

"Whatever you say, Father."

"You can go now, Lester," Hastings said. "Thank you for bringing my things."

"Anytime, Father, anytime."

Hastings opened the door to the outside and Lester stepped through.

"Father," he said, "if you do decide you want him killed, I can get it done cheap—"

"Good night, Lester," Hastings said. "Put any thoughts of murder out of your mind."

"Yes, Father. Good night."

Hastings closed the door and retrieved one of the cigars from the trunk. He lit it and sat at the table, savoring the taste and smell of the smoke.

He didn't think he was in any danger from Clint Adams. The man wasn't a bounty hunter, after all. More than likely he was simply riding through, and would be gone in a day or two. He saw no need to take any action at all.

Not yet, anyway.

FIVE

As Jack Odin had predicted, a couple of poker games did manage to break out, and Clint got into one. It was only after he sat down that he realized they were playing for nickels. He played for several hours and managed to win a few dollars before returning to the bar for a beer. He hadn't had one the whole time he was playing.

"I didn't say it was high-stakes poker," Odin told him as he set a beer down in front of him.

"No," Clint said, "you didn't."

"It passed the time, though, didn't it?"

"It did that."

"Of course," Odin said, "there are better ways to pass the time."

Clint turned to see where Odin was looking. The blonde, Beyla, was coming toward them. Clint had seen her working the room while he was playing poker. She had come over to him once to ask him if he wanted anything. She asked it with her hips pressed firmly to his arm.

"Nothing to drink," he'd said.

"Maybe later, then?" she asked. She had a husky voice that suited her.

"Yes," he said, "maybe later."

Now, as she approached, she folded her arms over her firm breasts.

"So, you decided to get a drink yourself, huh?" she asked.

"I, uh, finished playing and Jack here offered me—"

"How about buying me a drink, then?" she asked.

"Sure," he said. "Jack?"

"Beyla, Clint is a friend," Odin said. "There's no need to hustle him for drinks."

"Well," she said, "in that case give me a real drink instead of a watered-down one."

"Comin' up," Odin said. He brought her a shot glass of whiskey, and then left the two of them alone—as alone as they could be in the crowded saloon. They were, however, down at one end of the bar.

"So you and Jack are friends, huh?" she asked.

"Actually," Clint said, "we met today."

"Jack makes friends fast," she said. "So you're not from his O'Deen days, huh?"

"No," Clint said, "although I did hear that he had, uh, changed his name to suit him."

She laughed and said, "Jack changes everybody's name to suit himself. You'd better watch he doesn't try to change yours."

"To what?"

"Who knows?" she said. "One of those gods he's so crazy about."

"And you're not crazy about the Norse gods?"

"I don't know anything about them," she said, then gestured at the painting over the bar, "except for her."

"Freyja."

"Yes," Beyla said. "She's beautiful."

"So are you."

She looked at him and smiled.

"Thank you."

She sipped her whiskey.

"How long are you staying in town?" she asked.

"A day or two."

"Hmmm," she said, shaking her head.

"Why are you shaking your head?"

"I shouldn't be thinking what I'm thinking."

"And what are you thinking?"

"The same thing you're thinking," she said.

"And what's that?"

"You tell me."

"All right," he said. "I'm thinking that we shouldn't be wasting time."

She smiled and said, "That's what I'm thinking." She finished her whiskey and slammed the glass down on the bar. "So what are we waiting for?"

"Don't you have to work?"

"You heard Jack," she said. "You're a friend of his. He won't mind. Are you staying in his hotel?"

"I am."

"Let's go, then," she said, taking his arm.

They started for the door.

"Maybe I should know your name," she said.

He hesitated, then said, "It's Clint Adams."

She stopped abruptly.

"Is that a problem?" he asked.

"I know the name."

"And?"

She bit her lip, something he decided he wanted very much to do.

"What are you worried about?" he asked.

"I guess I, uh, just never been with a legend of the West before."

"You can drop that legend stuff," he said. "I'm just a man."

"A man people like to shoot at," she said.

"Oh, I see," he said. "You're not impressed, you're just worried someone will try to kill me while we're together."

"I just don't want to die by accident," she said. "You can understand that, can't you?"

"Sure," he said, "I understand. We can just call it off—"

"No," she said abruptly, "that's not what I meant at all."

"Then what did you mean?"

"I just meant that you should go on to your room," she said, "and I'll come a few minutes later—uh, if I don't hear any shots. Is that . . . fair?"

He laughed and said, "It's fair enough. I'll see you in a few minutes, then."

He was still laughing when he went out through the batwing doors and headed for the Midgard Hotel.

SIX

When Clint got back to the room it occurred to him that he might have put himself in a position to be set up. He didn't know Jack Odin, and he knew the woman called Beyla even less. What if she knocked on his door and had a few men in the hall with her? What if the idea of robbing a man with a reputation, or even killing him, appealed to her even more than sharing a bed with him?

This kind of thinking could be called two things: paranoid, or cautious. Clint didn't think he had reached the point in his life yet where he was paranoid, so he decided to be cautious.

His window overlooked the street, so he stood at it and watched for Beyla. He hadn't seen her in the street when there was a knock at the door. He drew his gun and went to it.

"Who is it?"

"It's me," she said in a loud whisper.

Clint turned the knob slowly and opened the door, standing off to the side just in case someone fired through it.

"I'm alone," she assured him.

"I was just—" he started, but she finished for him.

"Being careful," she said. "So was I, that's why I came the back way."

That explained why he hadn't seen her.

"Can I come in?"

"Oh, sure."

He stepped away from the door to let her enter. She missed only half a step when she saw the gun in his hand.

"You can check the hall," she said. "I'm alone."

"I believe you."

She laughed.

"Go ahead, check it. I won't be insulted."

He looked out in the hall, both ways, and found it empty. He stepped back into the room and closed the door.

"See?" she said. "Now we've both been careful, and here we are."

Somewhere along the way she had acquired a shawl, and now she took it off to once again reveal breathtaking cleavage.

"I didn't bring anything to drink," she said.

"We don't need anything to drink," he said.

They stared at each other for a few moments, and then Clint undid his gun belt and hung it on the bedpost.

"I get the feeling that's as much of a vote of confidence as I'm going to get," she said.

"I'd be hanging it there even if you weren't here," he assured her.

She walked up to him, then turned and looked over her pale shoulder at him.

"I have some buttons in the back."

He undid the buttons and parted the dress, revealing the lovely line of her back. He slid the dress down from her shoulders, where it bunched at her waist. He ran his hands over the skin of her back, and her shoulders, and then around to the front to cup her heavy breasts. She leaned back against him as his thumbs found her nipples, and they hardened immediately beneath his touch. He kissed her neck, and she let her head lean over to one side. He kissed her shoulder, nibbling on her a bit while he continued to knead her breasts.

"Wait," she said, stepping away from him abruptly.

"What is it?"

She turned to face him with her arm out, palm flat against his chest, as if to measure the distance between them.

"This is crazy."

"What is?"

Her eyes were wide as she stared at him. He guessed her age to be in the late twenties, so she was no wide-eyed virgin. There was something else going on here. He looked at her breasts and knew that in her thirties she'd be fighting to keep them from sagging beneath their own weight. At the moment, though, they were ripe-looking, like two luscious fruits.

"I'm out of breath already," she said.

"That's good," he said. "I'll take that as a compliment. Do you want to go slow?"

"This will sound silly to you," she said. "I've been with a lot of men . . ."

"I figured."

". . . and you've been with a lot of women . . ."

"Yes."

"But I think something special is going to happen here tonight," she finished. "Does that sound . . . silly?"

"No."

"I want to take it slow."

"All right."

"First," she said, "I have to get this off."

She wrestled the dress down to the floor and stepped out of it. She was wearing shoes with high heels, and she kicked them off. She was also wearing dark stockings, and he watched with enjoyment as she slid them off, and then her undergarments. Finally, she was fully naked and stood before him, breathing heavily.

"I haven't been this excited since . . ."

"Since what?"

"Since I lost my cherry," she said. "I was fourteen. That was more than half my life ago. I never thought I'd feel like that again."

Clint hoped she was telling the truth, and that she was not just telling him what she thought he wanted to hear.

"It's time for you to undress," she said.

"Yes."

"Do it slow, so I can watch."

She licked her lips, and from the way she watched him as he removed his clothes he was convinced that she was on the level. He was also convinced of something else.

She was right.

It was going to be a special night.

SEVEN

They met in a hot embrace and sank to the bed while in the midst of a long, searching kiss. Clint maneuvered Beyla so that she was on her back, then began to explore her body with his hands and mouth.

He went slow because that was what she wanted. He kissed her neck and shoulders, the slopes of her breasts, the undersides, teased her nipples by touching only the dark aureole with the tips of his fingers and his tongue, before finally taking them into his mouth and sucking them. While he did this his hand traveled down over her belly into the tangle of hair between her legs, which was even blonder than the hair on her head. He stroked her gently, probed lightly, until she was wet, and then he ran his finger along the wetness, but did not poke inside of her.

"God," she said finally, "stop teasing me."

"You said you wanted to go slow."

"You're sadistic," she said. "I want you inside me."

He straddled her then, and she grabbed for him and pulled him roughly to her. The tip of his hard penis touched her and then slid into her easily. She gasped, brought her legs up and around him, and they began to move together. They went slowly, at first, searching for

29

the proper rhythm, and when they found it they began to move faster and faster until Clint was gritting his teeth, trying to hold back, but her hands were on his buttocks, raking his back, her mouth was on his neck and shoulders, and finally he could hold back no longer . . .

"You call that slow?" he asked her, moments later.

"We can go slow next time," she said, gasping. "Where did you learn to tease a woman like that?"

"Practice," he said, "long years of hard practice."

"I'll bet!"

She turned on her side and began to stroke his flaccid penis. He started at her touch, because he was still sensitive.

"Are you going to tell me your real name?" he asked her.

"Why?"

"Well, Beyla isn't your name. Do you want me to keep calling you that?"

"Why not?" she asked. "What's the difference? You'll be gone tomorrow, or the next day. Why should you have two names to try to remember? Beyla is good enough."

"It's a pretty name."

"Yes, it is. Oh, look . . ." she said.

He looked, but he didn't have to. He could feel his penis hardening to her touch.

"Are you ready so soon?" she asked.

"Probably not," he said. "I probably need a little more help."

"I can do that," she said, smiling, and slithered down his body until she was lying between his legs.

"Mmmm," she said, taking him in her fists and pumping him, "there you go. Is that what you need?"

"Mmmm," he replied in kind, "that's nice, but I probably need just a little more help than that."

"I think I have just the thing," she said, and before he knew it he was in her hot, avid mouth. Her head moved up and down and from side to side while she held his testicles in one hand and stroked his shaft with the other.

Suddenly, she slid her hands beneath him to cup his buttocks and increased the tempo of her head, then decreased and took longer, slower mouthfuls of him, sliding her lips up and down the wet, slick length of him. She touched the spot between his balls and anus and he jumped, and then suddenly he erupted and she kept him in her mouth, kept sucking until he was totally empty, until there was nothing left to give. . . .

"Angela."

"What?"

"My real name is Angela."

It was a couple of hours later and he didn't know how she knew he was awake. Maybe it was his breathing. After they had made love for a second time they had both fallen asleep. He thought it odd that they had awakened at the same time, when it was still dark, still night.

"That's a name that shouldn't be changed," he said.

"Well," she said, "it didn't fit in with what Jack was trying to do."

"And the three of you didn't mind when he renamed you?"

"Why should we mind? It's his place, and he's paying us. Besides, he changed his own name, too."

"Changing from O'Deen to Odin isn't much of a stretch," Clint said.

"Maybe not," she said, snuggling closer to him, "but what the hell. Who knows how long we'll be here?"

"Do you want to leave?"

"Eventually," she said. "I don't want to spend my whole life here."

"And the other girls?"

"Same thing. It's like any other job, temporary."

"Do you share his feelings about this town?"

"You mean that it will someday build itself up again?

No, and I don't think he really believes it, either. He just doesn't want to admit that he picked the place to build his little empire, but now he's stuck with it.''

"Why?"

"Because he sunk every penny he had into this town, and his businesses. He can't sell it and make his money back, so he has to sit on his little man-made throne in his man-made Valhalla and hope for the best. The other girls and me, we don't have to do that.''

"Why don't you all leave together?"

"We agreed not to do that,'' she said. "That wouldn't be fair to Jack.''

"So you all stay?"

She shrugged and said sleepily, "We can't seem to decide which of us should leave first.''

EIGHT

Carmen Montoya sat at the front window of her father's house and stared out at the darkness. She didn't want to be here, she wanted to be with Father Frank. No, she *had* to be with Father Frank. That was where the Blessed Virgin wanted her to be.

Behind her, her family sat at the kitchen table, eating dinner. Her father, Eusebio, her mother, Consuelo, and her two older brothers, Carlos and Eduardo.

"It is not right," Carlos said.

"It is a sin," Eduardo said, "that is what it is."

"Be quiet," Eusebio said.

"They are right, my husband," Consuelo said. "Carmen should not be sharing a bed with a man of God."

Eusebio looked up from his bowl and found three pairs of eyes on him. They all knew that his daughter was his favorite, but how could he defend her against this?

Wearily, he tried.

"We do not know that she is sharing his bed."

"Ha!" Eduardo said.

"What else can she be doing there all night?" Carlos demanded.

"Praying," Eusebio said. "Perhaps they are praying."

"They are not praying," Eduardo said.

33

"But I am sure Carmen is on her knees," Carlos said.

"Carlos!" Consuelo said.

"It is true, Mama," Carlos said. "You know it is, even if Papa will not admit it."

"Finish your dinner," Consuelo said to her sons. "There will be no more talk."

By the window Carmen listened to her family talk about her. They did not understand. She was not lying with Father Frank because she lusted after him. She was doing it because the Blessed Virgin came to her in a dream and told her that she must. Why was this so hard to understand? She had told her mother about the dream, and her mother had slapped her face.

"How dare you!" her mother had said. "Why would the Blessed Virgin tell you such a thing?"

"I do not know, Mama," Carmen had answered. "It is not for me to question the Blessed Virgin."

"Your dream was nothing but an undigested bit of food," Consuelo had said, but Carmen knew the truth.

She went to Father Frank that very day and told him.

"Carmen," he said, "I don't think—"

"It is not for us to question, Father," she had said. "It is what I must do."

They were in his room, behind the church, and abruptly she pulled her peasant blouse down so that her full breasts bounced freely into view. She knew from the look on Father Frank's face that he wanted her, so she quickly undressed. Once she was naked, he could not resist, and she was in his bed from that day on.

Behind her, dinner was finished, and her brothers left the house, each throwing her a dirty look.

"Carmen?"

It was her father, coming up behind her.

"Papa?"

"Come and eat some dinner."

"I cannot, Papa," she said. "I am not hungry."

Eusebio looked behind him, to see if his wife was within earshot.

He leaned forward and said into his daughter's ear, "Why don't you go to him, then?"

"He told me to stay away tonight," she said. "I will go back tomorrow."

"So for tonight you just sit in the window? And stare outside?"

She looked over her shoulder and smiled at her father. It was he who understood the dream, and not her mother. She had found this very strange.

"I am fine, Papa," she said. "Do not worry."

"Ha," he said, "it is a father's job to worry."

"I am doing the Blessed Mother's bidding," she said. "No harm will befall me. She will protect me."

"Yes," Eusebio said, "she will." He leaned over and kissed his daughter's cheek. But would the Blessed Virgin protect his daughter from the thoughts and deeds of her own brothers, and perhaps even her mother?

Eusebio knew that his wife considered what Carmen was doing a grave sin. He just did not know what she would do about it as time went by.

Consuelo watched her husband and daughter from across the kitchen. She could not have been more disgusted by what Carmen was doing if she had been sharing a bed with her own father. That would also have been a sin, but at least it would not have been sacrilege.

Consuelo knew that the Blessed Virgin would never have told her daughter to do what she was doing. That meant that she, Consuelo, was going to have to pray to the Blessed Virgin for guidance. She could not allow this sin, this sacrilege, to go on. Something had to be done, and she knew her husband would do nothing. Carmen was his baby, his favorite, and he would never think badly of her.

If Consuelo was going to take some action she was

going to have to rely on her sons. They recognized the sin in what their sister was doing, even if Eusebio did not.

When the time came, she would at least be able to rely on her sons.

NINE

Clint woke the next morning to find Beyla—Angela—between his legs, nuzzling him.

"Do you mind?" she asked.

"It's my favorite way to wake up," he said.

She smiled, licked her lips, and then took him into her mouth. She sucked him until he was hard as a rock and then straddled him and sat on him, taking him deeply inside of her. She rode him up and down while he squeezed her breasts, popping the nipples between his fingers, and then he sat up so they could kiss while she continued to bounce up and down on him.

Abruptly he put his hands beneath her arms and lifted her, depositing her on her back so that he was now on top. He got up on his knees, grasped her ankles, and spread her legs apart widely, and began to pound her that way, in and out, in and out, faster and faster until he became mindless in his search for his own release. This was a selfishness he did not often allow himself, but this morning he wanted it, and he took it. . . .

Beyla/Angela dressed while Clint watched her.

"I think I'll call you Angela," he said. "I like it better."

"Better call me Beyla when we're at the saloon," she said. "Jack prefers it. If you call me Angela you'll shatter his fantasy."

"I wouldn't want to do that."

She came to the bed when she was dressed and kissed him warmly.

"Will you stay one more day?" she asked.

"At least."

She smiled and said, "Good. I'll see you later, then?"

"Definitely."

She flounced out the door happily, and he put his hands behind his head and stared at the ceiling. He had nowhere to go, really, no deadline of any kind. He felt pleasantly fatigued. What was the harm in staying another day? Or even two? Valhalla had suddenly become a much more interesting town to him. And he still wanted to go over to the Mexican side to see what that was like.

He thought about going back to sleep, but his stomach was demanding attention. He decided to get up and eat, and then to have a bath. After that he'd take a walk to the Mexican side and satisfy his curiosity about that.

TEN

He got up, got dressed, and went downstairs to the dining room. He'd wondered what he'd find when he got there, but other than the fact that the decor was much like the lobby, and the Asgard Saloon, it looked much like any other dining room. There were a few other diners there, and waiters working the floor, dressed the way waiters should be dressed.

"Good morning, sir," one waiter said, approaching him. "Are you a guest?"

"Yes, I am."

"What room, sir?"

"Seven."

"This way, then."

He followed the waiter to a table.

"Each room has its own table?" he asked.

"Of course, sir."

How very San Francisco, he thought, as he sat down. Maybe that was where Jack O'Deen—alias Odin—should have opened his hotel and saloon. Clint thought that he'd ask Odin about that when he saw him. He thought that the "Odin" act, along with all the Norse mythology, would probably go over very well in San Francisco's Portsmouth Square.

He ordered steak and eggs for breakfast, and a pot of coffee. While he was drinking his coffee he saw a man with a badge enter the dining room, and he knew instinctively that the man was looking for him. With all his interest in Jack Odin and his mythology, he had completely forgotten to check in with the local law.

The man looked around the room, saw him, and approached his table.

"Are you Clint Adams?"

"I am."

"Mind if I have a seat?"

"Not if you introduce yourself, I don't."

"Sheriff Wade Kantrell is my name."

"Well, have a seat, Sheriff, and some coffee, if you've a mind to."

There was another cup sitting upside down on the table so the sheriff righted it and said, "Don't mind if I do," pouring himself a cup.

Clint studied the man for a few moments. He was in his late thirties, maybe early forties, solid but not fat, cleanly dressed and well-manicured, a man who cared about his appearance.

"What can I do for you?"

"I heard you were in town," Kantrell said, "and was wondering why."

"Just passing through. I was planning on coming to see you later today."

"That so?"

Clint nodded.

"I usually check in with the local law," he said, "but yesterday just seemed to get away from me."

"Heard you spent a lot of time at the Asgard."

"Checking on me?"

"You're a known man," Kantrell said. "People see where you go. Guess you met that madman O'Deen, since you're staying in his hotel and spent time at the saloon."

"What makes him a madman?"

"This," Kantrell said, "all of this stuff about the gods. It's crazy."

"Is it?"

"It is to me," Kantrell said. "I never even heard of any of this stuff until he started it."

"Well," Clint said, "he didn't exactly start it. It goes back a long way."

"You heard of it?"

"Yes."

Kantrell shook his head.

"Still seems like foolishness to me."

"One man's foolishness . . ." Clint said.

"Huh?"

"Never mind. How long have you been sheriff here, if you don't mind my asking?"

"About five years."

"Then you were here before Odi—O'Deen."

"Way before."

"What about the other side of the river?" Clint asked. "You law for both sides?"

"Naw, they got their own law over there," Kantrell said. "A Mex name of Montoya is *el jefe* over there. Been there as long as I been here."

"Who's got more problems?"

"Ha!" Kantrell laughed. "He's married and has got three grown kids, one the prettiest Mex gal you'd ever wanna see. I'd say he's got more problems than me."

"His kids give him grief?"

"The gal," Kantrell said, "she's the one. The boys are hard workers, from what I hear."

"What kind of trouble is she?"

"I probably shouldn't be telling you this," Kantrell said, looking around to see if anyone else was listening, "but she's sleeping with the local padre."

"She's sleeping with the priest?" Clint repeated, surprised.

"That's what I said."

"Does the church know about this? I mean, his superiors?"

"Can't say I know one way or the other," Kantrell said. "I guess if they did know they'd yank his ass out of here, wouldn't they?"

"I'd think they would."

"Well, maybe they don't know." He finished his coffee and stood up. "How long you plan on staying in Valhalla?"

"Another day or two," Clint said. "Why don't I check in with you before I leave?"

"I'd appreciate that," Kantrell said. "Appreciate you staying out of trouble while you're here, too."

"I always try, Sheriff."

"Guess I can't ask more than that," Kantrell said. "Enjoy our town, what there is of it."

Clint watched the sheriff leave, and then the waiter arrived with his breakfast. The steak was cooked to perfection and he applied himself to his meal. Afterward he'd walk over to the Mexican side of town. It sounded like a very interesting place.

ELEVEN

When Clint reached the Mexican side of the walking bridge he saw a sign that said, in English: WELCOME TO SANTA MARIA. He wondered, if the American side was called Valhalla and the Mexican side was called Santa Maria, why anyone even pretended anymore that they were the same town.

Walking through town he was surprised to discover that Santa Maria seemed to be cleaner, and busier, than Valhalla. While there were no buildings like the Asgard Saloon and the Midgard Hotel, most of the buildings seemed to be in better condition than most of the buildings in Valhalla. Clint realized that he had assumed that the Mexican side would be even more run-down than the American side.

It was a wrong assumption to have made, and he felt badly about it.

He stepped into the first cantina he saw and ordered a beer. When it came it was warm. That was one assumption he'd made that turned out to be right. Mexicans, he had always noticed, seemed to enjoy warm beer—at least, when they were in Mexico.

"You are a stranger in town, señor," the bartender said.
"Yes."

"Are you staying in town?"

"Yes," Clint said. Then, "Well, no, I'm staying across the bridge, in Valhalla. I'm, uh, not sure if that's the same town or not."

"Many people are not sure of that these days. Perhaps I can help you with something?"

"With what?"

"With whatever you need," the man offered.

The cantina was empty this morning, so maybe the portly, balding bartender with two gold teeth simply wanted someone to talk to.

"I don't really need anything at the moment."

"But perhaps later you will?" the man asked. "A woman, perhaps?"

"No," Clint said, "I don't need a woman."

"A boy, perhaps?"

Clint gave the man a hard stare.

"I won't need a boy!"

"Very well," the bartender said, backing away, "then perhaps the señor only needs directions?"

Clint was about to ask, "To what?" when he realized that he did need directions.

"All right," Clint said. "Could you direct me to the church?"

"The church?" the man asked, stroking his jaw. "*Sí*, if you like I can direct you to the church. Eh, why would you want to be going to the church?"

"I just want to see it."

"It is not a very big church," the man said, "or a very nice one."

"That's okay," Clint said. "I don't want to buy it, I just want to look at it."

The man started to laugh.

"You are very funny, señor," he said. "Of course I know you don't want to buy the church. Who would want to do such a thing?"

And he laughed some more.

Clint waited until the man stopped laughing to speak again.

"All right," he said, "will you direct me to the church?"

"*Sí*, señor," the man said, and did so. They were not difficult directions to follow.

"Thank you."

"Do you know Father Frank?"

"Who?"

"The priest," the man said, "Father Frank. Do you know him?"

"No, I don't," Clint said. "What's he like?"

"He is the kind of man, señor," the man said, "that some people like, and some people don't like."

"That sounds like any man," Clint said.

"Well," the bartender said, "I do not think that Father Frank is like any man."

"Then he's special?"

"I would not say special," the man replied. "I would say . . . different. He is different from other men."

"Well, he's a priest."

"Ah," the man said, raising a finger, "but he is different than other priests."

Clint wondered if what the sheriff had told him that morning was general knowledge, or just a piece of information that he happened to have.

"How is he different from other priests?" Clint asked.

"In many ways."

"Name one."

The bartender straightened up.

"It would not do for me to talk of a man of God behind his back."

"But you brought it up."

"Perhaps señor would prefer to see for himself."

"I guess I'll have to," Clint said, "if you're not going to tell me."

"I cannot," the bartender said. "It would not be . . . proper."

"But you were talking about him a minute ago."

"But no longer," the man said, and walked to the other end of the bar.

The conversation was apparently over. Clint left the remainder of his warm beer and walked out of the cantina.

TWELVE

Clint followed the bartender's directions and found the church. Although not a large building, the white adobe structure seemed firm enough. He could see from where he was standing that there was no bell in the bell tower.

He heard something and turned to see a small boy approaching. The boy stopped right next to him, staring at the church.

"Hello," he said.

"*Buenos días,*" the boy said.

"Do you speak English?"

The boy, who appeared to be nine or ten, looked up at him and nodded.

"What's your name?"

"Luis."

"Well, Luis, my name is Clint. Do you know Father Frank?"

"*Sí,*" the boy said, "I know the padre."

"Do you like him?"

The boy nodded enthusiastically.

"Why?"

"He is different."

Well, he'd heard that before.

"Do you mean different from other men, or different from other priests?"

The boy seemed to put a great deal of thought into the question, and then confidently announced, "Both."

"And have you heard this from your parents? Your mama and papa? Or from other grown-ups?"

"*Sí*," Luis said, "but I have also seen it for myself."

"And what have you seen?"

"Father Frank has legs."

"He has . . . what?"

"Father Frank, he has legs." The boy touched his own legs, and then patted Clint on one of his to make his point further.

"What do you mean?"

"Priests and nuns do not have legs."

Suddenly, Clint thought he knew what the boy meant. Priests and nuns usually wore long, flowing robes that covered their legs. A child might therefore think that they did not have legs.

"Have you seen Father Frank's legs?"

"Yes."

"How?"

"I have looked in his window."

"And what else did you see?"

"I cannot say."

"Why not?"

"It is a secret."

"Who told you it was a secret?"

"Father Frank."

"When?"

"When he caught me looking in his window."

"Ah . . ."

"Do you know Father Frank, señor?"

"I've never met him."

"Are you here to kill him?"

"Now, why would I be here to kill Father Frank?"

The boy shrugged.

"Is Father Frank expecting someone to come and kill him?"

Again the boy shrugged.

"Or is that part of the secret?"

This time the boy did not react at all.

"Well," Clint said, "if it's a secret I won't ask you about it anymore."

"Señor, I have a sister."

"You do?"

He nodded.

"Older or younger?"

"Older. Would you like her?"

"Would I . . . like her. You mean, if I met her, I'd like her?"

The boy shook his head.

"For two pesos she will give you the suck job."

"The suck job?"

The boy nodded, then held both hands out in front of him like he was grasping something tubular.

"Never mind," Clint said, slapping the boy's hands down.

"For three pesos she will lie in bed with you."

"Luis," Clint said, "I don't think I want to buy your sister."

"She is not very pretty, it is true," Luis went on, "and she is missing some teeth," and now he held his hands out in front of him in a universal gesture, "but she has very big—"

"Never mind!" Clint said, cutting him off. "I'm sure your sister is very nice, but I don't want to buy her. Why don't you run along now?"

"If you change your mind," the boy said, "just ask anyone for Luis. Everyone knows me."

"I'll remember that, Luis. Thanks."

The boy turned and walked off a few feet, then turned back.

"Father has a gun in his trunk," he said, then turned and ran. "He is truly God's favorite."

A gun in his trunk? A priest who slept with women and had a gun. What would Mother Church think of this? he wondered.

THIRTEEN

Frank Hastings saw the man standing outside the church, talking to little Luis Castanon. Hastings knew Luis because he had caught the boy looking in his window one night while he was in bed with Carmen. Carmen hadn't seen him, so she didn't know what was happening when Hastings left the bed and went to the door. It took a lot of talking on Hastings's part to try to explain to the boy what he saw. As it turned out, the boy was not at all upset or surprised to see Hastings in bed with a woman. Rather, he was shocked to have seen that Father Frank had legs.

Hastings knew exactly what Luis meant when he said that. It was something he himself had heard when he was smaller, only about nuns.

"God thinks very highly of me, Luis," Hastings had said to the boy, "that he gave me legs, like other men."

"But you are not like other men," Luis had said. "You are a priest."

"I am one of God's favorite priests, Luis," Hastings had said. "Always remember that."

Of course, Hastings still had no idea that Luis had returned the next day and sneaked into his room. He did not know that the boy had looked in his chest and seen the gun and holster, among all the other things that were there.

Luis became convinced that Father Frank was God's favorite priest, because not only had God given him legs, but a gun as well.

Now Hastings watched as Luis walked away from the man, who he knew was Clint Adams. He had seen Adams once, a long time ago, and the man had not changed very much.

Despite the fact that Clint Adams—the Gunsmith—was standing outside the church, Hastings still did not think that the man had come looking for him.

Of course, there was only one way to find out for sure.

Clint studied the church from the outside, and finally decided to go on in and take a look. He started for the building, and as he approached it the doors suddenly opened and a man appeared in the doorway. He was wearing a priest's traditional robe.

"Can I help you, my son?"

"You were watching me?"

"I saw you watching the church," Hastings said. "I sensed you were hesitant to enter. I was about to come out and get you. Are you troubled about something?"

"Actually," Clint said, "no, I'm not. I just wanted to take a look inside the church."

"Come in, then," Hastings said, stepping aside. "Everyone is welcome to the house of God."

Clint entered and Hastings left the church doors open and followed.

"It is a modest church," he said.

Clint silently agreed. It was small and plain.

"I noticed there was no bell in the bell tower," Clint said.

"Alas," Hastings said, "our bell cracked, and we haven't the money to buy a new one."

Clint turned to look at Father Frank. He couldn't shake

the feeling that there was something familiar about the man.

"You're an American."

"Yes, I am."

"Isn't it odd for an American priest to be in a Mexican church?"

"This is a Catholic church," Father Frank said, "not a Mexican church. There's a difference."

"Of course there is," Clint said. "I'm sorry."

"Mother Church sent me here to look after the souls of these people," Hastings said. "It didn't matter to me that it was in another country."

"I guess it shouldn't."

"Now you have seen the church," Hastings said. "Is there anything else I can do for you? Do you have something you wish to ask me?"

"I'm actually just sightseeing, Father," Clint said. "I'm staying in Valhalla, but everyone on this side of the river seems to want to help me."

"Ah," Hastings said, "then I guess Luis offered you his sister?"

"He did."

"You turned him down, I hope."

"I did," Clint said, "although he made her sound . . . interesting."

"Interesting," Hastings said, smiling, "is not the word I would use to describe Luis's sister. Who else has been helpful?"

"The bartender in the cantina," Clint said. "He offered me a girl, and then a boy."

"And you did not take him up on either?"

"No, I didn't," Clint said. "Like I said, I'm just sightseeing."

"I'm sorry I have no more to show you," Hastings said, "except for my own room, in the back."

"No," Clint said, "I don't need to see that, thank you. I guess I'll leave and let you get on with your work."

Hastings walked Clint to the door, and they both saw the girl approaching the church. She was beautiful, and Clint wondered if this was the girl the sheriff had said the priest was sleeping with.

"Carmen," Hastings said. "Come in, my child." The priest looked at Clint and said, "Confession."

"I understand, Father," Clint said. "Thanks for letting me look around."

"Anytime."

Clint stepped aside to let the beautiful young woman enter, and then stepped outside. The doors to the church closed behind him.

FOURTEEN

Hastings and Carmen walked to his room. Once inside Hastings discarded the robe.

"Who was that man?" she asked.

"Just a man."

"He looked dangerous."

"I'm sure he is."

She looked at his table and the paper that was on it.

"More poems?"

He walked to the table and gathered up the sheets of paper.

"Yes."

"May I read them?"

"No," he said, "not these."

"As you wish," she said, looking chastened.

He walked to her and tilted her chin up with his hand so he could look into her face.

"The day will come when I will let you read some of the poems, Carmen," he said. "I promise."

"Yes, Padre."

"How is your family?" he asked.

"They hate me."

"They don't hate you."

55

"Yes, they do," she said, "but it does not matter. I do what must be done."

"I'm sure your father does not hate you."

She smiled then, but it slid away quickly.

"No, he does not."

"You are his favorite."

"Yes."

"And your brothers?" Hastings asked. "How are they treating you?"

"They do not speak to me."

"And your mother?"

"She speaks to me all the time. She tells me what a sinner I am, and that I will go to hell."

"Your mother should come and see me."

Carmen shook her head.

"She will not. They will not come to church."

"Yes, I know," Hastings said. "I'm sorry. It's my fault your family does not come to church anymore. That is on my head."

"No, Father Frank," she said, taking his hand and kissing it. "You are good."

Hastings looked at her and thought that she was probably the only person, in his whole life, who had ever said that to him.

FIFTEEN

Clint left the church and walked back through Santa Maria until he came within sight of the bridge to Valhalla. He wondered if Jack Odin would call it Bifrost, the Rainbow Bridge.

As Clint was approaching the bridge a man stepped between him and it. He was wearing a badge and a sombrero. As he got closer the man slipped the sombrero from his head, and it hung behind him.

Clint stopped.

"You are Clint Adams, señor?"

"That's right."

"I am *el jefe* here," the man said. "My name is Montoya."

"Glad to meet you."

"I would like to buy you a drink, señor."

"Unfortunately," Clint said, "I was on my way back to the other side."

"Your return to your country will have to be . . . delayed, until after we have talked."

Clint stared at the man.

"Oh, I know you could shoot me down, señor, and walk over my body, but I do not think you would do that."

"Just where do you want to buy me this drink?" Clint asked.

The man brought his left hand up and Clint saw the bottle he was holding.

"Right here, señor," Montoya said, "and then you can go back over the bridge."

"Okay, then," Clint said. "Let's do it."

They walked away from the bridge and leaned against a nearby buckboard. Montoya uncorked the bottle and passed it to Clint. The sheriff was in his early fifties, but was tall and well put together. Clint remembered what his American counterpart had said about the man having troubles.

Clint took the bottle, drank from it, and passed it back. Montoya took a longer swig, and Clint could tell from the color in the man's face that it was not the first of the day.

"What's on your mind, Sheriff?"

"Did you go to the church?"

"I did."

"And you met Father Frank?"

"Yes."

"I have a daughter," Montoya said.

"I heard you had three children."

"You are well informed, señor," Montoya said. "I have two sons and a daughter. My sons, however, are hard workers."

"And your daughter?"

Montoya handed him the bottle.

"She is something of a problem."

Clint drank and passed it back.

"In what way?"

"She makes a poor choice of men in her life."

"And what does that have to do with me?"

"I thought perhaps you could help me in this matter."

"And how would I do that?"

"By killing the man she has chosen."

"Why don't you do it?"

"I cannot."

"Why?"

"I cannot kill this man," Montoya said, and took a long drink.

"Again," Clint said, "why not?"

"Because he is a man of God."

"The priest?" Clint asked in surprise. "So your daughter really is sleeping with the priest, Father Frank?"

Montoya hesitated, made a face that revealed the torment he was going through, and said, "Yes."

"Then I saw her today," Clint said. "A very beautiful girl of about nineteen?"

"That is her," Montoya said. "She was with him?"

"She came to the church as I was leaving."

"Señor," Montoya said, "this is a very unusual priest."

"So I've been told."

"By who?"

"The bartender at the cantina," Clint said, "and a little boy named Luis."

That made Montoya laugh.

"Luis? Did he try to sell you his sister?"

"He did."

"She is one ugly *puta*," Montoya said, "but she has very big—"

"So he told me," Clint said. "Sheriff, I don't think I am the man to help you."

"But are you not the Gunsmith?"

"I don't hire my gun out."

"I see."

"Do it yourself."

"I cannot kill a priest."

"Not even one so unusual?"

"Señor, he is a countryman of yours. Did you know him when you saw him?"

"No, I didn't," Clint said. "Why? Should I have?"

"It is very strange," Montoya said. "He came here

some months ago, supposedly sent by Mother Church to replace our beloved Father Cisco, who died. He was quite old.''

"So now you have a younger priest."

"Now we have a strange priest," Montoya said, "one who has taken my daughter to his bed."

"Can't you talk to her?"

"I have," Montoya said. The bottle was hanging forgotten from his fingers. "So has her mother."

"And what does—what's her name?"

"Carmen."

"What does Carmen say?"

"She says the Blessed Virgin came to her in a dream and sent her to Father Frank."

"And do you believe that?"

"I believe that she believes it."

"Maybe it's Father Frank you should talk to."

"I already have. He says he cannot send her away when she comes to him."

"Then you do have a problem."

"I am afraid, señor," Montoya said, "afraid of what my wife, and my sons, might do."

"You mean your wife might send your sons to kill the priest?"

"It is a possibility."

Clint could see where that would put the man in a tight spot. He was the sheriff, and if his sons committed murder, what was he to do?

"I'm sorry, Sheriff," Clint said, "I still can't help you."

Montoya sighed and shook his head.

"I must solve this dilemma myself, then."

"I'm afraid so."

"Go, señor," Montoya said. "Go back to your side of the bridge. I will not try to stop you."

Clint stood up.

"The problem is mine," Montoya said, and suddenly

he sounded very drunk. "A strange priest, one who sleeps with my daughter, and writes poetry . . . strange man . . ."

Clint left the sheriff muttering to himself and went back across the bridge to Valhalla.

SIXTEEN

When he reached the other side there was another man with a badge blocking his path.

"Welcome back," Kantrell said, his arms folded across his chest, as if he was keeping his hands as far away from his guns as he could. "Was it interesting?"

"Very."

"I see you had a conversation with Montoya."

"Yes," Clint said. Kantrell fell into step with him and they started walking back into town. "He confirmed what you told me about his daughter sleeping with the priest."

"I told you he had more problems than I did," Kantrell said.

"You weren't kidding."

"What did he ask you to do?" Kantrell asked. "Kill the priest?"

Clint almost answered the question, but then decided he shouldn't be telling one lawman that another lawman had tried to hire him to commit murder—not even if the other lawman was from another country.

"He just wanted to talk."

"He didn't try to hire you?"

Clint looked at Kantrell.

"What kind of lawman do you think would try to hire me to commit murder?"

Kantrell snorted and said, "The desperate kind."

"I'm afraid my conversation with Sheriff Montoya is between me and him."

"Fair enough. What did you think of Santa Maria itself?"

"Lots of friendly, helpful people," Clint said. "I was also surprised at how clean it was."

"Cleaner than here, huh?"

"Yeah, and it also seemed busier."

"Yeah," Kantrell said, "I'm afraid our two little towns are going in opposite directions."

"Two little towns?"

"I'm one of those people who admits that we're not one big happy town anymore."

"Were you ever?"

"Not happy, no."

They were approaching the hotel, but Clint was not heading there.

"Can I buy you a drink?"

"A beer would be nice," Clint said. "A cold one."

"Sure. That's the one thing we still have over Santa Maria," Kantrell said, almost proudly. "Cold beer."

"That's a big something," Clint said.

SEVENTEEN

If nothing else the walk over to Santa Maria had proven to Clint that cold beer was better than warm beer—as if that point needed to be proven.

"Did you meet the priest?" Sheriff Kantrell asked.

"Yes, I did."

"What did you think of him?"

Clint thought a moment.

"He didn't stand like a priest."

They were standing at the bar and Clint turned to face Kantrell.

"What did he stand like?" Kantrell asked.

Clint hadn't realized it at the time, but now that he said it, it made sense.

"He stood like a man wearing a gun."

"Why would a priest wear a gun?"

"Why would a priest sleep with a woman?" Suddenly, the vision of Carmen Montoya came into Clint's mind. "Never mind, forget I said that."

"Maybe he had a gun on under his robe?"

"I don't think so," Clint said. "I might have noticed that. No, I think he stood like a man who was used to wearing a gun."

"Well," Kantrell said, "you're the expert. You'd know."

"What's going on?" Jack Odin asked, coming over. It was early and there wasn't much business in the place.

"We're talking about the priest in the church across the bridge," Kantrell said.

"Father Frank? What about him?"

"Clint met him today."

Odin looked at Clint.

"He's a nice fella."

"You've met him?" Clint asked.

"Sure," Odin said, "I've been to his church."

Kantrell frowned at Odin.

"I thought you didn't believe in God," he said. "I mean, in one true God?"

"I never said that."

"But what about all this?" Kantrell waved both arms about.

"This is just stuff I'm interested in."

"Then you do believe in God?"

"I didn't say that, either."

"Then what are you saying, Jack?"

"All I said was, I've been to his church, I've met the man, and he seems like a nice fella."

"You know he's sleeping with the sheriff's daughter over there, don't you?"

"Hey," Odin said, "more power to him. I've seen her, too."

"But he's a priest!" Kantrell said.

"He's still a man," Odin said.

"He's playing with fire," Kantrell said. "Those Mexicans don't like anyone—especially gringos—messing with their women."

"Is she complaining?" Odin asked.

"That don't matter," Kantrell said. "Her family's complaining. Her father just tried to hire Adams to kill him."

"Hey, hey," Clint jumped in, "I never said that."

"You didn't have to," Kantrell said. "I know Eusebio Montoya, and I know that his wife keeps after him about things that bother her—and this bothers her."

"You aren't going to do it, are you?" Odin asked.

"Even if he did make the offer," Clint said, "I don't hire my gun out to anyone."

"Well good," Odin said. "I'd hate to see Father Frank catch a bullet."

"Maybe he wasn't always a priest," Kantrell said.

"What are you talking about?" Odin asked.

"Clint said he stands like a man who used to wear a gun," Kantrell said. "Maybe he did wear a gun once."

"He'd have to have worn it a long time to still be standing like he was wearing one," Clint said.

"So maybe the priesthood came to him late in life," Kantrell said. "Are you allowed to do that? Join up after you've already, uh, lived a life?"

"I don't know," Clint said.

"Maybe he's killed people," Odin said. "Would they take him if he'd killed people?"

"I don't know," Clint said again. "I'm not an expert on the church."

Odin and Kantrell continued to debate whether the church would take a man who had once killed people when suddenly Clint tuned them out and remembered something Montoya had said. He'd been rambling, but he said something about Father Frank writing poetry.

That struck a chord in Clint's mind, and he carried his beer to a table to think about it.

EIGHTEEN

"You look like you're very far away."

Clint looked up and saw Beyla looking down at him.

"I came in early to see if you were here," she explained. "Can I sit down?"

"Sure."

She sat across from him.

"What are you thinking about?"

"I went over to Santa Maria today."

"Uh-oh," she said. "Did you meet one of those dark-haired, Mexican beauties?"

"No," he said, "well, yes, sort of, but that's not what I was thinking about."

"Then what *were* you thinking about?"

"A priest."

"Oh," she said, "you mean Father Frank."

"Yes. Do you know him?"

"Never met him," she said, "but we hear a lot about him on this side."

"Like what?"

"Oh, like stuff you've probably already heard. About him sleeping with a woman, although I don't know which one. I've always been curious about that."

Clint didn't say anything, and suddenly Beyla sat forward.

"You know, don't you?"

"No."

"Liar," she said. "Come on, tell me."

"You have to promise not to tell anyone else."

"I promise."

"Not even your Norse sisters."

"I swear."

"Well," he said, "apparently, it's the daughter of the sheriff over there."

"Wow," she said. "He's looking for trouble doing that, isn't he?"

"I would say so."

"Did you meet him today?"

"I did."

"What'd you think?"

"That's the problem," he said. "I didn't think much about him when I met him, but since then . . ."

"What?"

"Well, there's just something familiar about him, something nagging at the back of my memory."

"You think he's not who he says he is?"

"Maybe . . ." He explained about Father Frank standing like someone who used to wear a gun.

"How does someone stand like they're wearing a gun when they're not?"

"The gun is a weight on your hip," he said, "and it's a weight you get used to carrying with you. Some men, when they stop wearing a gun, still move as if that weight is on their hip."

"So you think he was a gunman in this country? Did he go to Mexico to hide?"

"It could be," he said. "I've known other men who have gone south of the border to hide out, but none of them ever became priests before."

"Oh."

"And none of them wrote poetry."

"What?"

"Sheriff Montoya said that Father Frank writes poetry," Clint explained.

"So?"

"That rings a bell with me."

"A gunman who wrote poetry?"

"Yes."

"That's . . . weird."

"I just can't place it in my head."

"Maybe you know somebody who could?"

"Yes," he said, "as a matter of fact, I do. Does this town have a telegraph office?"

"Sure, but—"

"I've got to go."

"Will you be back later?"

"Sure I will."

"And will I, uh, see you after I get off?"

"I'll be here, Ang—I mean, Beyla. I've just got to send a telegraph message before the office closes."

She gave him directions and he left the saloon, waving at Jack Odin as he went by the bar. The sheriff had left some time ago.

"Coming back?" Odin called.

"Soon," Clint said in mid-wave and went out the door.

NINETEEN

Clint got to the telegraph office in plenty of time to send a telegram to Rick Hartman, in Labyrinth, Texas. If anyone would have a memory of a poetry-writing gunman, he would.

Clint worded the telegram carefully, gave it to the clerk, and paid for it.

"Where will you be for the reply?" the man asked.

"The Asgard or the Midgard."

The clerk shook his head and was saying something about "weird names" as Clint went out the door.

Jerry Gates and Al Waxx stopped their horses in front of the sign that said VALHALLA.

"What the hell does that mean?" Waxx asked.

"Who knows?" Gates replied. "It's just the name of a town."

"It's a weird name," Waxx said. "I thought you said there was a town here called—what'd you say it was called?"

"It don't matter," Gates said. "This is it, and this is where we're supposed to meet the others."

"Are they gonna know this is it?" Waxx asked. "What if they just keep riding?"

"Where?" Gates asked. "Into Mexico? Sammy ain't that dumb."

"He ain't?"

"Well," Gates said, "between him and Dave they'll figure it out."

Sammy Martin and Dave Barrett were supposed to meet Gates and Waxx here, and they were supposed to plan what their next robbery was going to be.

"Wonder if this town's got a bank," Gates said aloud. He favored robbing banks over trains or coaches. Banks weren't moving.

"We ain't gonna find out sitting out here," Waxx said. "Come on, let's go."

"Val-halla," Gates said. "You're right, it's a weird name for a town—but I like it."

"I don't," Waxx said, as they started their horses forward again.

"You know what your problem is?" Gates asked.

"What?"

"You got no imagination."

"Why do I need imagination?" Waxx asked. "You got enough for both of us."

TWENTY

When Clint left the telegraph office he figured he had two choices. He could go back to his hotel, where he'd sit in his room alone, or he could go back to the saloon, where at least he'd have someone to talk to.

It wasn't a hard decision.

When he got to the Asgard Saloon, business had become brisk. The other girls had arrived and were working the floor along with Beyla. Clint went to the bar and stood a few feet down from two strangers who were working on beers. When Jack Odin saw him he drew a beer and carried it over.

"What took you out of here so fast?" Odin asked, handing him the beer.

"I had a telegram to send."

"About the priest?"

Clint nodded while he took a small sip of beer. He still managed to drop some from his chin.

"What about him?" Odin asked, leaning on the bar.

"It's the poetry thing," Clint said.

"And not the fact that you think he used to wear a gun?"

"Lots of men used to wear a gun," Clint said, "but how many write poetry?"

75

"I don't know—" Odin said, but Clint interrupted him by snapping his fingers.

"Wait a minute!" he said.

"Something come to you?"

"It's not writing poetry," Clint said, "it's reading it."

"I don't get you."

"I'm not thinking of a gun hand who wrote poetry, but one who read it."

"And who was that?"

Clint paused a moment, groping, then shrugged and said, "I still can't think of his name."

"Excuse me."

It was one of the strangers talking.

"Yes?" Clint asked.

"I'm sorry, but I couldn't help overhearing your conversation. Are you trying to think of the name of a man who made his way with a gun and read poetry all the time?"

"I am," Clint said. "Why? Does that ring a bell with you?"

"Well, I knew a fella once," the man said, "his name was Hayes—"

"That's it," Clint said. "Frank Hayes, wasn't it?"

"That's right," the man said. He and his friend moved in closer, and Clint suddenly realized that they had the look of a couple of hard cases.

"My name's Gates, and my friend's name is Waxx," the man said. The other man nodded. "Do you know Frank Hayes?"

"I don't know him," Clint said. "I've heard of him. He was supposed to be good with a gun."

"Oh, Frank was good with a gun, all right," Gates said. "Maybe the best I ever seen. Would you, uh, happen to know where he is right now?"

"Nope," Clint said.

"But you were talking about him."

"Something the bartender said made me think of poetry, and that made me remember Hayes—although I couldn't come up with his name until you said it.''

"Uh-huh,'' Gates said. "So you haven't . . . seen him, maybe around here, lately?''

"I told you,'' Clint said. "I never met the man.''

"Yeah, that's right,'' Gates said. "You did say that. Sorry. Like I said, I didn't mean to interrupt, but I thought I heard you talking about . . . a friend.''

"Sorry I can't help you,'' Clint said.

"That's okay.''

Gates and Waxx moved down the bar some, even further away than they had been before.

"What was that about?'' Odin asked.

"I'm not sure,'' Clint said, "but I think I might have just gotten Father Frank in trouble.''

"Father Frank's last name isn't Hayes.''

"What is it?''

"It's Hay . . . stings—oh.''

"Yeah,'' Clint said, "oh.''

TWENTY-ONE

"Do you think you should go warn him?" Odin asked.

"I'm not even sure it's the same man."

"What's the harm, then?" Odin asked. "If it's not, then he doesn't need to be warned. If he is, then it'll do him some good."

"I suppose . . ."

"What if they are friends of his, though?" Odin asked.

"Look at those two," Clint said. "Do they look friendly to you?"

Odin looked down at the two hard cases and said, "No, they don't."

"I don't recognize either of them," Clint said, "do you?"

"Never saw them before."

"I wonder what their business is in town."

"Maybe the same as yours."

"It could be," Clint said, "but maybe it's for the sheriff to find out."

"He should be doing his rounds soon," Odin said.

"Well, maybe I should talk to him even before that."

"Leaving again?" Odin asked, but Clint was already gone.

• • •

"He's leaving," Waxx said. "You think he's gonna warn him?"

"We don't even know if he's really in town," Gates said.

"Why would this fella be talking about Hayes if he ain't in town?" Waxx said. "That son of a bitch, I can't wait to get my hands on him—"

"You'll have to wait," Gates said.

"How long?"

"Until the others get here," Gates said. "They got as much right to him as we do. He ran out on all of us."

"And took the money with him," Waxx said.

"You know," Gates said, "if Hayes wanted to get out of the business I don't have a problem with that—but to take all that money with him? That I can't stomach, or forgive."

"I can't either," Waxx said. "Do you think he still has the money?"

"Oh," Gates said, "if I know Frank Hayes, he's still got most of it."

"Good," Waxx said, "then we can take back however much he has left."

"And then the rest," Gates said, "out of his hide."

Clint found Sheriff Kantrell in his office, looking as if he was about to leave.

"I was just going to start my rounds."

"I want to talk to you about something first."

"Is it important?"

"It could be."

Kantrell rested a hip on his desk.

"Okay, go ahead."

"There are some strangers in town."

"I'll check them out."

"Well, yes, that's what I was getting at, but I may have accidently caused some trouble."

"For who?"

"Father Frank."

Kantrell stood up.

"Take that up with Sheriff Montoya."

"I will," Clint said, "but first I think you should check these fellas out."

"I said I would." Kantrell frowned. "What kind of trouble are you talking about, here?"

Clint told the sheriff about his conversation with Odin, and how the two strangers had chimed in and become very interested.

"Do you think Father Frank is this Frank Hayes?" Kantrell asked.

"I can't be sure," Clint said. "I never saw Frank Hayes, and I only met Father Frank recently."

Kantrell rubbed his jaw.

"What do you know about Hayes?"

"Only that he made his way with a gun."

"Would I have any paper on him?"

Clint shrugged.

"I can't say. If he rode with these two fellas, maybe. They look like the type who'd be wanted."

"I'll talk to them," Kantrell said, "and take a look at them, and then I'll come back here and check my wanted posters."

"And if they're wanted."

"I'll take them in," Kantrell said. "Don't worry, Adams, I'll do my job—"

"I wasn't questioning that," Clint said. "I was just wondering what you'd do if Father Frank turned out to be Hayes, and you did have some paper on him."

"He's in Mexico," Kantrell said, "out of my jurisdiction. I'd do the only thing I could do."

"Which is?" Clint asked.

"I'd have to tell my colleague, Sheriff Montoya, that his priest is a wanted man."

TWENTY-TWO

They agreed that Clint would go back to the saloon first. They also agreed that he would not interfere while Kantrell was questioning the men.

"No problem there," Clint said. "I don't want them knowing I went to you, anyway."

The two men were in agreement, so Clint left. Kantrell said he'd be along in about twenty minutes, in the course of his regular rounds.

When Clint reentered the saloon he was glad to see the two men still standing there. Odin, seeing him come in, beckoned to him.

When Clint reached the bar Odin handed him a telegram.

"This came for you while you were gone."

"Did you read it?"

Odin looked chastised.

"I had to see who it was for."

Clint read it. It was from Rick Hartman, telling him what he already knew. There was a gun hand who read poetry by the name of Frank Hayes, but not one who wrote it.

Clint put the telegram in his pocket and accepted a beer from Odin.

"Looks like Father Frank's your man," the big bartender said.

"Not my man," Clint said around a swallow of beer, "but maybe theirs." He indicated the two strangers.

"You talk to the sheriff about them?"

"Yes," Clint said. "He'll be along shortly to check on them. Maybe he can get them to move along, or find out their business."

"Seems to me that's his job, anyway," Odin said.

"I guess so."

"You gonna warn Father Frank?"

Clint looked at Odin for a moment.

"Seems to me he deserves a warning," the bartender said.

"Seems to me you may be right," Clint said, "much as I'd like to stay out of it."

"Well," Odin said, "I'd go, but I'm not really welcome on the Mexican side."

"Why not?"

Odin made a face.

"Long story. A misunderstanding, really."

"About a woman?"

Odin smiled.

"What else?"

"Don't worry about it," Clint said. "Since it was my big mouth that may have caused him the trouble, it should be me who lets him know about it."

Clint nursed his beer until the sheriff entered. It was more like forty minutes than twenty, but the two men were still there, still at the bar. When the sheriff came in they were talking with the dark-haired girl, Roskva. In ten minutes she had gotten them to buy her two drinks and another beer each. She stared up at them with big, beautiful brown eyes and let them look down her cleavage. She was very good at her job.

The sheriff exchanged a glance with Clint as he walked

by him and waved at Odin. Both the bartender and Clint watched as he reached the two men, shooed Roskva away, and engaged them in conversation. It seemed to be a very easy talk with no tension on either side. All three men nodded, and then the sheriff came over to where Clint was standing, but spoke to Odin.

"How about a beer, Jack?"

"Comin' up, Sheriff."

He looked at Clint and nodded, as if simply exchanging a polite hello. When Odin brought him the beer, he leaned over it and talked to Clint that way.

"So?" Clint asked.

"They say they're just passing through, not looking for trouble," Kantrell said.

"What do you think?" Clint asked.

"It seems to me they're waiting for someone."

"Why do you say that?"

"Well, they're just passin' through, but they don't know when they're gonna leave. I just got the feeling they might be waiting for someone else to get here."

"You can't get them to move on?" Odin asked.

Kantrell looked at Odin but was actually speaking more to Clint.

"They haven't done anything that I can kick them out of town for."

"I'm going to go over and warn Father Frank tomorrow," Clint said.

"That might start trouble," Kantrell said, "not stop it."

"He's got a right to know," Clint said. "Besides, if there is trouble it will probably be on the other side of the border."

"You have a point," Kantrell said. He straightened, drained his beer, and put the empty mug on the bar. To Odin he said loudly, "Back to my rounds. I'll see you later."

He turned and said quickly to Clint, "Stay out of trouble."

"My middle name," Clint responded, and the sheriff left.

TWENTY-THREE

Clint remained at the bar until the two men decided to leave. They walked unsteadily past him and did not pay him any mind. Odin called Roskva over and asked her about them.

"Drifters," she said, "and probably outlaws. They were trying to impress me."

"Did they say where they were staying?" Clint asked.

She looked at him and smiled. He had the feeling the three girls had talked about him.

"They're not at the Midgard, I know that," she said. "I think they're at one of the rooming houses."

"Okay, Roskva, thanks," Odin said. "Back to work now."

"Yes, Boss."

She gave Clint one last smile and one last look at her cleavage before leaving.

"Doesn't that feel silly to you?" Clint asked.

"What?"

"Calling her Roskva, or calling the others Beyla and Sif?"

Odin frowned.

"What's silly about it?"

"Never mind," Clint said. "I'm going to my room to get some rest."

"You mean, until Beyla gets there?" Odin asked, grinning.

He had definitely been talked about.

"Good night," he said.

"Be careful out there," Odin said. "You don't know what those two have in mind."

"They have Frank Hayes in mind," Clint said, "not me."

"I'd still be careful."

"I always am."

Clint left and had an uneventful walk back to his hotel.

A few hours later, when there was a knock at the door, he answered it, thinking it was Beyla. It was a woman, but not her. It was the smaller, darker, paler Roskva.

"Hi," she said.

"Hi."

"I have a message from Angela. Can I come in?"

"Sure," Clint said, and backed away to admit her.

Roskva was dressed much the way Beyla had been the night before, still wearing her dress, but with a shawl over her shoulders and bosom.

"Is something wrong?"

"No, nothing," she said, smiling. "We three girls just had a talk and we decided that Angela shouldn't get too attached to you, since you'll be leaving soon."

"I see. So she's not coming."

"No, but I'm here."

"To deliver the message."

"Well," she said, taking her shawl off and tossing it away, "to deliver . . ."

Roskva was small but energetic. She had small breasts, like hard little peaches, with large and responsive nipples, and she had a wonderful, almost plump butt that her dress kept hidden, but was in plain, glorious sight in bed.

At first Clint was tentative, but when Roskva removed her dress and pressed her naked body against him while rubbing his crotch, any tentativeness disappeared.

She pushed him down on the bed and mounted him quickly. It was while she was riding him that he discovered how sensitive her nipples were. He squeezed her breasts and pinched her nipples, and when he brought them to his mouth and bit them she nearly went crazy. She began to bounce up and down on him like a madwoman, and he had no choice but to recline and try to stay with her. Just as he was about to explode inside of her he felt her tremble and then she shouted loud enough for anyone outside the room—and maybe the hotel—to hear. . . .

"I'm sorry," she said later, while lying on the crook of his arm.

"About what?"

"I'm loud," she said. "I know that."

"It's okay."

"I mean, I'm only loud when it's really good, you know?"

"That's good," he said. "I'll be able to tell when I'm not doing my part."

"Oh," she said, "you'll do your part. We have all night."

"All night?"

She nodded.

"Angela said that you were . . . up to it."

"That's the second time you've called her Angela."

"We don't use Jack's names for us between us, just when we're working."

"So what's your real name?" he asked.

"Rose," she said. "Not such a stretch from Roskva, I guess."

"How do you feel about Jack changing your names?"

She shrugged and said, "It's his place, and he pays us. He can call us whatever he wants."

"Tell me something, Rose."

"What?"

"How did you end up being the one to . . . deliver the message tonight?"

"We drew straws," she said. "I won. Actually, I cheated, but don't tell Amy."

"Amy?"

"She's Sif."

"Oh."

"Actually," she said, "if you stay another night Sif will come over. That's so I don't get too attached to you, either."

She started to drift off to sleep and he thought, Hell, what's another night?

TWENTY-FOUR

Rose was up first in the morning, and she woke Clint by climbing on top of him and rubbing her wiry pubic hair up and down the length of his penis. When he was awake and she was wet, she slid him inside of her and rode him until she was sweating and he was gritting his teeth, trying to hold back. Finally, he couldn't, and in one, long, explosive moment it was over. . . .

"I smell like a goat," Rose said, dressing while he watched. "You look like you're enjoying that."

"What?" he asked.

"Watching me dress."

He smiled.

"Just one of my small pleasures in life."

Fully dressed, she sat on the bed next to him.

"How many of those do you have?"

"A lot," he said. "Too many to count."

"And what was last night?"

He smiled.

"One of life's great big pleasures."

She leaned over and kissed him.

"Right answer. See you at the Asgard later?"

"I'll be in."

She kissed him again and left. He was impressed that she never asked if she'd see him after work.

But then again, tonight was for Sif, wasn't it?

After Rose/Roskva left he reclined for a few moments before rising, washing, and dressing. He went downstairs for breakfast and was shown to his table. When Sheriff Kantrell appeared he was not surprised.

"Pull up a chair," he said as the man reached his table.

"You don't seem surprised to see me."

"I'm not."

Kantrell sat down, made a face, and poured himself some coffee.

"I hate being predictable," he said.

"So do I," Clint agreed, "but sometimes it's unavoidable. We weren't able to speak freely in the saloon last night. I figured I'd see you here."

"Mind if I eat while I'm here?"

"Not at all."

Clint waved and the waiter came and took the sheriff's order.

"So what did you think of our two friends?" Clint asked.

"I went back and checked them for paper," Kantrell said.

"Find any?"

"No," the lawman said, "but I know it's out there. I can feel it. Their names are Gates and Waxx. That ring a bell with you?"

"No."

Clint was becoming more and more impressed with Kantrell, who had not made a very strong first impression. He smelled something wrong about those two men, as well.

"You think they're actually here looking for Frank Hayes?" Kantrell asked.

"No," Clint said. "They seemed . . . surprised to hear

his name, but they were very interested. No, I don't think
they came here looking for him, but I think they are looking now.''

"Are you going to go and see him today?"

Clint nodded.

"Right after breakfast," he said, just as the waiter arrived with his meal. It took a few minutes before the man
returned with Kantrell's.

"What about Montoya?" Kantrell asked.

"What about him?"

"Are you going to warn him that there might be trouble
in his town?"

"I suppose I should."

"Well, if it was me, I'd sure appreciate it."

"Then I guess I'll tell him. Let me ask you a question?"

"Sure."

"Do either you or Montoya ever cross over into each
other's, uh, jurisdiction?"

"Never."

"What happens if some Mexicans come over here and
start trouble?"

"That depends on the degree of trouble we're talking
about," Kantrell said. "I'll likely throw them in jail and
then send them back over if no one's been hurt and nothing's been stolen."

"And does he operate the same way?"

"Yep."

"And this is an agreement the two of you have?"

Kantrell thought a moment, then said, "I guess it is."

"What do you mean, you guess it is?"

"Well, we haven't spoken to each other in some time."

"How long?"

"Let me think . . .'' Kantrell concentrated on his breakfast for a few moments before coming up with an answer.
"Oh, it's probably been . . . almost five years."

"That seems odd."

"Does it?"

"Well, you're sheriffs in what are essentially neighboring towns. I would think you'd get together more than that."

"Well," Kantrell said, "I never go over there, and he never comes over here."

"Is that something you've agreed—never mind," Clint said. "Forget I asked."

"I only hope that the problems he's having with his daughter don't affect his judgment."

Remembering the state the man was in the last time they spoke, Clint hoped the same thing.

TWENTY-FIVE

Clint and the sheriff left the hotel together and went their separate ways. Clint walked to the bridge and crossed into Santa Maria. He was halfway into town before he made his final decision about who to talk to first. He changed direction and headed for the church.

Frank Hastings woke with the pleasant weight of Carmen on his shoulder. She was lying on his right side, his right arm beneath her, which was something he never would have allowed as little as a year ago. In fact, he was awake only a few moments when the pleasant weight suddenly became an oppressive weight. Gently, so as not to wake her, he slid his arm from beneath her and left the bed. She stirred for a moment, moved a bit, then settled back to sleep.

Father Frank dressed and left the room, entering the church. He walked to the front pew and sat down, staring up at the crucifix. It had been months since he had come across the dead priest who'd originally been on his way here. The letter in the man's pocket had explained where he was going and what his duties would be when he got there. In that moment Frank Hayes ceased to exist, and he became Father Frank Hastings. The funny thing about it was, Frank Hastings was the dead priest's real name. If Frank Hayes was going to pick an alias, it certainly would not have been something so close to Hayes. It was for that reason that he told people almost immediately to call him Father Frank.

Although he certainly would have picked the name Frank for himself.

But the disguise of the priest was too good to pass up, even with the similarity in names.

Carmen was something he hadn't counted on at all, but she was also something that was too good to pass up. Luckily, the people in town were so religious that anything their priest did was fine with them. After all, he had not only been sent by Mother Church, but also by the Virgin, and by Jesus Christ.

In addition to all that, Father Frank had actually been a godsend to these people. Since he couldn't say mass—there was no way he could fake that—he had instituted something new. He spent all day Sunday in church and was available to anyone who wanted to talk with him about their troubles. In the beginning he had used Carmen as a translator. That was how he met her. Little by little, though, he began to learn the language. Amazingly, after four months, he was able to speak Spanish fluently.

Frank was amazed how at peace he felt here, but he knew it could not last. He was, after all, a priest who did not say mass, who slept with a beautiful young Mexican girl. How long would it be before someone said something, before Mother Church found out what was going on?

How long would it be before *someone* found him?

At that moment he heard the church doors open, and the morning light flooded in. He turned and saw a man silhouetted in the doorway. He was wearing a gun on the right side. Like many moments before during the past four months, Frank's mouth went dry. He had just been wondering when he'd be found, and now he thought of his gun in the trunk in his room.

"Father Frank?" the man called.

Frank recognized the voice, and the man. It was Clint Adams.

"Mr. Adams?"

"That's right."

"Come in, please."

Clint looked around the church.

"Do you think we could talk outside?"

Frank walked toward Clint.

"Does it make you uncomfortable being in the house of God?"

"Considering what we have to talk about, Mr. Hayes," Clint said, "I would think we'd both be uncomfortable in here."

There was a tense moment between them, and then Father Frank said, "By all means, let's step outside."

TWENTY-SIX

He didn't bother to deny it.

"How did you find out?" he asked when they were outside. "Do you know me from somewhere?"

"No," Clint said. "I know the name, and your . . . interest in poetry."

"A silly interest for a man in my business," Hayes said. "Or rather, the business I *was* in."

"But you only read it back then," Clint said.

"Now I write it," Father Frank said. "Even sillier."

"Not so silly."

Father Frank looked up at the sky, then back at Clint.

"You didn't tell me how you found out."

"I'm kind of embarrassed about this."

"Why?"

"I think I've put you in a bad position."

"Maybe you'd better explain that."

Clint did, starting from the beginning, the nagging feeling that he couldn't pin down. He finally got to the part about the two strangers, and when he was finished Father Frank nodded.

"Jerry Gates and Al Waxx."

"That's what the sheriff said. I didn't know the names."

"Were they alone?" the phony priest asked. "I mean, just the two of them?"

"Yes," Clint said, "but the sheriff over there and I feel that they might be waiting for someone."

"I'm sure they are," Father Frank said. "They're probably waiting for Sammy Martin and Dave Barrett."

"I don't know them, either."

"You wouldn't," Father Frank said. "Of the five of us I was the only one foolish enough to maintain a high profile."

"I know what that's like."

"Yes, you would."

Clint studied the man standing before him and was struck by how peaceful his face looked.

"How long have you been here . . . I don't even know what to call you?"

"I've gotten kind of used to Father Frank. Would you like to walk?"

"Sure."

"I guess I owe you an explanation."

"After I may have put you in danger?" Clint asked. "Why would you owe me an explanation?"

"Maybe because you also decided to warn me. You could have just gone on your way and let whatever happens happen."

"No," Clint said, "I couldn't have."

Father Frank smiled and said, "See? That's why."

". . . decided I'd finally had enough," Father Frank finished. They had walked completely around the church several times by the time he got to this point, and they were now standing in front of it again. "I was going to get out."

"And you came here and became a priest?"

"That was an accident," Father Frank said, "or fate. You decide."

He went on to explain about finding the dead priest and taking his place.

"How did he die?"

"Apparently he'd fallen from his buckboard and hit his head," Father Frank said. "I buried him, dressed in my clothes, and I put on his clothes and came here to do what the letter said."

"Which was what?"

"Provide guidance and comfort to these people, and let them know that God and the Church will always be with them."

"And have you done that?"

"Surprisingly," Father Frank said, "I believe I have."

"You seem very . . . peaceful."

"I am that, too."

"And what about your gun?"

"It's in a trunk, in my room."

"You haven't gotten rid of it?"

"I . . . tried several times, but couldn't."

"Well, it might be good that you didn't, considering."

"You might be right."

"What about the girl?"

"I thought you might ask me that."

"Well," Clint said, "as I understand it, your relationship with her is very unpriestlike."

"Yes," Father Frank said, "it is, but I simply could not resist her."

"She seduced you?"

"Yes."

"She's very . . . young."

"And she was inexperienced," Father Frank said. "Still, she was the one who came after me. She has the idea that God wants us to have this relationship, that while I offer comfort to all of the people who live here, she offers comfort to me."

"Well," Clint said, "I'm sure she does that."

"I know it can't go on," Father Frank said. "I *knew*

it wouldn't last, but I was hoping for more time.''

"Well, you may have it," Clint said.

"What do you mean?"

"Gates and Waxx don't know you're here," Clint said. "I mean, here on this side of the border, here in the church. Maybe they'll meet with the other two, look around, not find you, and leave."

"Who else knows about this?"

"Sheriff Kantrell, and Jack O'Deen, who owns the hotel and saloon in Valhalla."

"I've met O'Deen," Father Frank said. "He calls himself Odin, you know, after the Norse god."

"Yes."

Father Frank shook his head.

"False gods," he said.

"Spoken like a true priest."

"Sometimes," Father Frank said, "I think I am."

"Except for the girl."

"Yes."

"And the money."

Father Frank seemed to freeze for a moment, then he looked at Clint.

"What money?"

"Come on, Frank," Clint said, dropping the "Father." "Those four wouldn't be so anxious to find you after all this time unless you took off with some money, maybe the take from the last job you pulled."

"You're very good," Father Frank said.

"It just makes sense."

"Okay, yeah, I did take some money. I wish to Go— I wish now that I hadn't."

"Give it back."

Father Frank shook his head.

"You don't want to?"

"I can't."

"Don't you have it?"

"Sure, I do," he said, "almost all of it."

"Then what's the problem?"

"I know those four," he said. "Giving them the money won't satisfy them. They want to kill me."

"Then I guess you'll just have to hope that they give up and go home."

"I don't know what the chances of that are," Father Frank said. "Now that they've gotten wind of me, they may not give up so easily."

"Only time will tell, I guess."

"I think you're right."

"You'll have to stay out of sight for a while."

"That won't be a problem," he said. "I don't usually go far from the church."

"What about supplies?"

"I have . . . people who bring me what I need."

"Like tobacco? Maybe some cigars and whiskey?"

Father Frank gave Clint a stunned look.

"I haven't been watching you," Clint said. "There are just things I think you would miss while trying to live a celibate—or not so celibate, but different—life."

"You're right, of course," Father Frank said. "I don't know how real priests do it."

"They're dedicated, devoted men," Clint said.

That remark seemed to bother Father Frank.

"Yes," he said, "yes, I suppose they are."

TWENTY-SEVEN

Before Clint left, Father Frank told him to come back sometime.

"It will be nice to talk to someone who knows the truth, I think."

"That might not be a good idea," Clint said.

"Why not?"

"I might be followed."

Father Frank smiled.

"I think you could manage not to be if you wanted."

Clint said he'd see about it, and the two men shook hands. Father Frank went back into the church, and Clint headed back to Valhalla. He didn't know when he had decided not to talk to Sheriff Montoya, but it seemed to him that doing that would only cause more trouble for Father Frank.

He was amazed at how easy it was for him to think of the former outlaw and gunman Frank Hayes as "Father Frank." He knew what it was like to have a reputation, and that was all he knew of Frank Hayes. He decided to judge the man on what he saw and not on what he'd heard.

It was what he wanted from people, and never got.

• • •

When Father Frank reentered the church he found Carmen standing there, looking worried.

"What did he want, Father?" She spoke to him in Spanish.

Try as he might he could not get her to call him by his first name. She did it every once in a while, but for the most part she addressed him as "Father."

"Just to talk."

"About what?"

He kissed her forehead and said, "Only things that don't concern you, Carmen. Don't worry."

"I do not want to see you hurt."

"Why would anyone hurt me?"

"Because you are a good man," she said. "The bad— the *evil*—are always looking to hurt the good."

He put his arms around her and drew her to him for a comforting embrace, nothing more.

"I promise you," he said, "no one is going to hurt me."

"I will not let them," she said fervently. "I would kill them first."

"You are not going to kill anyone, Carmen," he said, holding her tighter. "There will be no need for that— ever! That I promise you."

Clint was approaching the bridge when he saw the one man he'd been trying to avoid: Sheriff Eusebio Montoya.

"Sheriff," he said, nodding. "Is this what you do? Guard the bridge?"

"I saw you in town, señor," Montoya said, "only then—poof—you were gone."

"Just wanted another look around," Clint said. "It's a nice, clean little town."

"*Sí*, señor, it is," Montoya said, "and I would like to keep it that way."

The sheriff was sober today, and there was not a bottle in sight.

"What's your point, Sheriff?"

"My point, señor, is that I would not like you to come back to Santa Maria. I would like you to stay on your side of the bridge."

"And why's that?"

"Because I know your reputation, Señor Adams," Montoya said, "and I would not like anyone to try to shoot you on my streets."

Clint frowned at the man. It seemed to be gone and forgotten that just yesterday a drunk Montoya had tried to hire him to kill Father Frank. Maybe, he thought, now that the lawman was sober he was embarrassed by what had happened.

"Don't worry, Sheriff," Clint said, "I'm not looking for any trouble."

"Señor," Montoya said, "a man like you does not have to look for trouble. It finds you."

"I'll keep that in mind, Sheriff," Clint promised. "I'll keep that in mind."

TWENTY-EIGHT

When Al Waxx entered the room he shared at the rooming house with Jerry Gates, Gates was lying on the bed with his boots on, hands laced behind his neck.

"Where've you been?" Gates asked.

"Out walking," Waxx said. "I gotta tell you what I saw."

"What?"

"I saw that fella from last night coming over the bridge."

"From the Mexican side?"

Waxx nodded.

"I wonder what he was doin' over there?"

"That's what I was wonderin', too. Do you think Hayes is over there?"

"Maybe," Gates said, swinging his feet to the floor.

"And that fella was warning him?" Waxx went on. "If that happens Hayes might leave."

Gates sat there chewing his lip, as if he hadn't heard what his partner had said.

"Jerry? Whataya thinkin'?"

"I'm thinking we should find out who we're dealin' with, here," Gates said.

"You mean that fella?"

"That's who I mean," Gates said. "We got to find out his name."

"How do we do that?"

Gates stood up.

"We ask around, that's how. Come on."

They walked around town for a while, trying to find someone who knew who Clint was, but nobody did. Or, as far as they were concerned, no one was talking.

"What about that bartender?" Waxx asked. "We could ask him."

"He seemed friendly with the man," Gates said. "He probably wouldn't talk."

"We could make him."

"Did you see the size of him?" Gates asked. "Are you prepared to shoot him to make him talk?"

"Well—"

"I'm not," Gates said.

"We could ask the sheriff."

"Same answer," Gates said. "Besides, I don't want to go anywhere near the law."

"Then who else can we ask?"

Something occurred to Gates just then.

"Did you see him get a telegram last night?" he asked Waxx.

"No, I didn't."

"Well, I did. Come on."

It wasn't hard to make the telegraph operator talk. Gates and Waxx presented a menacing presence, and the man folded immediately.

"Sure," he said, "I remember that man. I took his reply over to the saloon."

"Right," Gates said. "And you keep copies of all the telegrams, right?"

"That's right, sir," the little man said. He was fighting to keep his knees from shaking. He was a middle-aged man who had never faced violence in his life, because he was always a clerk somewhere. These two men, however, were clearly ready to perpetrate violence against him if he didn't give them the right answer.

"Well, find that copy," Gates said.

"I'm, uh, not supposed to let other people see, uh, other people's telegrams. I could, uh, lose my job."

"You could lose a lot more—" Waxx started, but Gates cut him off.

"Mister, all we need is his name."

"Oh," the clerk said, "well, I guess there can't be any harm in that, can there?"

"Not if you give it to us," Waxx said.

"J-just a moment."

The man turned and walked to his desk, where he opened a drawer. He reached in, took out a few copies, found the one he wanted, read it, and then replaced it. He then went back to the counter.

"Well?" Waxx asked.

"Clint Adams?"

"What?" Gates asked.

"Uh, Clint Adams."

"Are you sure?"

"That's what he said—"

"Let me see that copy," Gates said.

"Sir, I can't—"

"Let me see the damn thing!" Gates shouted.

The man leapt into action, retrieved the copy, and handed it to Gates, who read it carefully.

"Here," he said, shoving it at the clerk. "Come on," he said to Waxx.

Waxx started to speak, but Gates was gone and Waxx hurried after him.

"What the hell is going on?" Waxx asked. "Was it Clint Adams?"

"Yes," Gates said.

"Well, shit," Waxx said, "the goddamned Gunsmith.

Hayes gets him on his side, there ain't gonna be nothing we can do.''

"Yes, there is.''

"What?''

"We wait for the others,'' Gates said. "I don't care if Clint Adams is on Frank's side, I still like four against two.''

TWENTY-NINE

Clint didn't want to see Sheriff Kantrell any more than he'd wanted to see Sheriff Montoya, so naturally the lawman was the first person he saw when he came back across the bridge and walked into town.

Kantrell was walking on the boardwalk across the street, passing in front of the general store, when he spotted Clint walking toward his hotel.

"Hey, Adams!"

Clint considered just walking on but decided against it.

Kantrell came across the street at a trot and joined Clint on his side.

"Just come back from Santa Maria?"

"As a matter of fact, I did."

"Going back to your hotel?"

"Yes."

"I'll walk with you," Kantrell said. "I want to hear what happened when you told Montoya the news."

"Actually," Clint said as they walked, "I didn't get a chance to."

"Why not?"

"I didn't see Montoya," Clint lied.

"Couldn't find him, huh?"

"That's right."

113

"I bet you saw the priest, though, didn't you?"

"As a matter of fact, I did."

"Did he deny who he was?"

Clint looked at Kantrell, wondering how serious the man was about never going over the bridge.

"No," Clint said, "he didn't deny it."

"How did he explain it, then?"

Clint made a quick decision not to tell Kantrell about the money. He was actually surprised at that moment because he realized he hadn't bothered to ask Father Frank how much money there was.

"He just decided to give up his old life and start a new one."

"As a priest?"

"That was an accident," Clint said, and explained how Kantrell happened to find the dead priest and change clothes with him.

"And you believe that?"

"Why not?"

"Because he probably killed the priest himself."

"I don't think so," Clint said.

"He's got you fooled."

"I don't think so . . ." Clint said again.

"How does he explain sleeping with a woman when he's supposed to be a priest?"

"Well," Clint said, "he's not a priest, is he?"

"But as far as those people know, he's supposed to be, right?" Kantrell asked. "How do they feel about it?"

"He's their priest," Clint said. "Apparently, whatever he does is all right with them."

"But not with the girl's family."

"They're upset, as you know."

"Then he'd better watch out," Kantrell said as they reached Clint's hotel.

Clint stopped right in the doorway and blocked Kantrell from entering.

"I'm going to go to my room for a while."

"I was on my way to do something, anyway," Kantrell said. "Maybe I'll see you later at the saloon."

"I'll be there," Clint said.

Kantrell nodded and started back up the street the way they had come. Clint waited a few moments to be sure the man wasn't coming back, then left the hotel and walked to the telegraph office. He wanted to send Rick a telegram asking how much he knew about Frank Hayes.

THIRTY

Clint noticed immediately that the clerk appeared nervous. He wrote out his message and watched as the man worked the key. From the way he was cursing and starting over, the clerk was obviously having a problem.

"Is there a problem?" Clint asked.

Immediately, the clerk turned and pleaded, "It wasn't my fault, you gotta believe me!"

"Calm down," Clint said. "If you made a mistake you can fix it."

"No, not this," the clerk said, indicating the key and then getting up from it. He came over to the counter, rubbing his hands together nervously. "I'm talking about those men."

"What men?"

"The two men who came here asking about you."

"Asking about me?"

The clerk nodded.

"When was this?"

"Earlier today."

"And what did you tell them?"

"I told them who you were," the man said. "I couldn't help it. I was frightened."

"Look," Clint said, "it's okay. Don't worry about it."

"Really?"

"Yes, really," Clint said. "Why don't you go and finish sending my message."

"You're not angry?"

"No, I'm not."

"I th-thought you'd be angry."

Clint kept his temper, because now he *was* becoming angry with the little man.

"I'm not," he said. "Send the telegram, and I'll leave and you can relax."

The clerk nodded, sat at the key, and began to operate it.

Clint realized that he had expected this. After the conversation they'd had, Gates and Waxx would naturally try to find out who he was. The question now was, what would they do, now that they knew?

"Oh," Waxx said, "there was something else I needed to tell you."

"What?"

They were in a small café they had found on a side street, having lunch.

"When Adams came back over the bridge he ran into the sheriff and they had a talk."

"About what?"

"I don't know."

"Where did they go?"

"I don't know."

"Didn't you follow them?"

"No."

"Why not?"

Waxx thought a moment, then shrugged and said, "I don't know."

"Then why was it important to tell me that?"

"I don't know."

"God," Gates said, "sometimes you're stupid."

"Hey—"

"Eat your lunch."

Clint stopped by the sheriff's office, half hoping the man wasn't there. Kantrell was too damned interested in what he was doing. The lawman was behind his desk.

"What are you doing here?"

"I just found out something you should know."

"What?"

"Gates and Waxx," Clint said.

"What about them?"

"They know who I am."

Kantrell frowned.

"How'd that happen?"

Clint told him.

"This could be trouble."

"Maybe," Clint said, "but probably not until their other two friends show up."

"I think you're right," Kantrell said. "The two of them aren't about to go up against you alone."

"Maybe I should just leave town," Clint said.

"Maybe they'd follow you."

"Or maybe they'd stay here and keep looking for Frank Hayes."

Kantrell chewed his lower lip for a few moments before he said, "How about some coffee?"

"I should be go—"

"I want to talk to you about something," the lawman said. "Have a cup with me?"

"Okay," Clint said, "sure."

"Have a seat," Kantrell said, getting up from his desk, "I'll bring it to you."

Whatever was on the sheriff's mind it must have been important, and he must have felt that Clint was going to say no.

He accepted the cup of coffee from Kantrell, who took his own and sat back down at his desk.

"What's on your mind, Sheriff?"

"I don't have any deputies—"

"No."

"Hear me out."

"I'm not wearing a badge."

"Hear me out, for Chrissake!"

Clint took a deep breath and let it out.

"Okay," he said, "I'm listening."

"I don't have any deputies," Kantrell started again, "and if Gates and Waxx are going to stay around and wait for their friends, there's bound to be trouble."

Clint remained silent.

"I'm not a fool," the sheriff went on. "I know my limitations. I can't handle the four of them. Heck, I probably couldn't handle the two of them."

"If they find Hayes," Clint said then, "the trouble will be on the other side of the border."

"But they're on this side now. And their friends will be on this side. I need backup, Adams, whether you wear a badge or not." Kantrell looked directly into Clint's eyes. "I'm askin' you not to leave town yet."

"All right," Clint said immediately.

"Just like that?"

"Sure," Clint said, "I wouldn't want anything to happen after I left that would be on my conscience." He sipped the coffee, then put the cup down on the desk. "Just like that, except for one thing."

"What's that?"

"Don't ever ask me to drink your coffee again."

The sheriff grinned and said, "Deal."

THIRTY-ONE

When Odin heard that Clint was staying, he announced that he was buying him a beer.

"Do you know that I've hardly paid for a beer since I got here?"

"That's why it pays to be friends with the boss," the bartender said, putting the beer in front of him. "We are friends, aren't we?"

"Sure we are," Clint said, picking up the beer. "Here's to friends."

"Wait, wait," Odin said. He grabbed a glass and a bottle, poured himself a shot, then raised it and said, "To friends."

They both drank.

"What happened with those two fellows last night?" he asked.

"That's why I'm staying," Clint said. "There's liable to be trouble. They're waiting for two more men."

"You know that for a fact?"

"Yes."

"And the sheriff asked you to stay?"

"That's right."

"How long?"

"I don't know," Clint said. "I guess until those other men get here."

"That could be a while."

"I don't think so."

"Oh," Odin said dejectedly.

"But it'll probably be for a few days, anyway."

"Well," Jack Odin said, "that's okay, then, isn't it?"

The place was almost empty, but there was a man at the other end of the bar who wanted service, so Odin went off to take care of him.

Clint wondered what he was going to do while waiting for Sammy Martin and Dave Barrett to arrive. He hadn't told the sheriff that he'd gotten their names from Father Frank. He didn't want Kantrell to know the depth of the conversation he'd had with the outlaw turned phony priest.

He thought about returning to the church as Father Frank had asked him to, for more conversation, but Sheriff Montoya had warned him off. He had to walk through part of the town to get to the church, so he didn't know if he could get there without being seen. At the very least, though, the man deserved some kind of progress report about his pursuers.

Clint decided that somehow he'd manage to get over to the church to keep in touch with Father Frank.

Odin came back to his end of the bar and leaned his elbows on it.

"So what are you going to do while you're waiting?"

"I don't know."

"You could play poker."

Clint made a face.

"Not for nickels."

"Well, you could just hang around here, then."

"And just drink beer and get drunk?"

"Who knows? You might get lucky with one of the girls."

Or two or three of them, Clint thought. Suddenly he

wondered what would happen after Sif came to him tonight. Would they start over again from Beyla?

He could think of worse ways to pass the time.

"You wouldn't mind that?" Clint asked.

"Hell, no," Odin said. "They're free to do what they want when they're done working here. Pick one out and try for her. Which one do you like?"

"They're all beautiful," Clint said.

"I saw the way you and Beyla were looking at each other the first day," Odin said. "What about her?"

"I'll have to think about it," Clint said. "I don't want to make a hasty decision."

"Suit yourself," Odin said. "Look, I've got to get the bar set up for tonight. I'll talk to you again later."

"Sure," Clint said, "go to work."

Clint looked down at his beer mug and knew that the one thing he couldn't do was hang around here and drink all the time. It wouldn't do to be totally drunk when trouble started. What kind of backup would he be for the sheriff then?

He decided to go outside, even if it was just to take a walk.

Sheriff Wade Kantrell sat in his office cleaning first his Winchester, and then the scattergun he kept on a rack on the wall. He hadn't had to use either weapon in a long time, and he wanted to be sure they were in working order.

He recognized the irony in asking Clint Adams not to leave town. At first he had thought that having Adams in town would cause trouble. Now he was asking the man to help him handle trouble.

How did this happen, anyway? Maybe it was Adams who had brought this on. After all, Gates and Waxx would probably have come to town, met their compadres, and then moved on. It was only overhearing Adams talking in the bar about poetry that had caused them to become potential trouble.

But who knew? Maybe when the other two men got there they would have tried to rob the bank. No, there was no use in blaming Clint Adams, not after the man had offered to leave town to avoid trouble, and then agreed to stay and help.

Kantrell shook his head. When this was all over he was going to have to get himself a deputy.

THIRTY-TWO

Clint took one turn around town and knew that staying in Valhalla was going to be rough. Maybe he'd be able to talk to Gates and Waxx and get them to leave. Before he tried that, though, he'd check with Father Frank and see if he thought there was any chance of that. Also, if he was going to do that he'd have to let Sheriff Kantrell know about it.

It was too late to go see Father Frank now, but first thing in the morning he would try to sneak over to the church without Sheriff Montoya catching sight of him. For now there was nothing to do but go back to the hotel, or the saloon. The question was, which one?

"I think we could take him," Waxx said to Jerry Gates.

They'd gone most of the day since lunch without talking about Clint Adams. Gates not only considered this statement stupid, but unnecessary.

"He'd kill both of us."

"Not," Waxx said, "if we bushwhacked him."

"And that would bring the law down on us."

"So we kill him, too."

"Why don't we rob the fucking bank while we're at it?" Gates asked.

125

"We could."

"You moron."

They were in their room, and at that moment Jerry Gates wished he had his own. He got up from the bed and went to the door.

"Where are you going?" Waxx asked.

"For a walk," Gates said. "Don't do anything until I get back."

Waxx sat on the bed.

"I'll just sit here and think."

"No!" Gates snapped. "That's the last thing I want you to do. It's too dangerous."

"But—"

"Take a nap, damn it," Gates said, "but don't do anything else."

He stormed out of the room and slammed the door behind him.

On the street Gates just walked, wondering why he even kept Waxx around. Maybe Frank Hayes had the right idea all along. Get away from men like Waxx, and get out of this life. Maybe that's what Gates would do himself—right after he killed Hayes and got the money back.

Gates decided to go to the saloon for a drink. How could he expect a moron like Waxx to understand that all of the success they'd had over the years was because they'd worked as a team? They were never more successful than when they were five, usually led by Frank Hayes. Since Hayes left Gates had tried to take over, but while they'd had some success, it just wasn't the same. For Waxx to think that the two of them could successfully do something was way beyond stupid.

He reached the saloon and entered. The first thing he did was look for Clint Adams. He spotted him easily, standing at the bar talking to the bartender. There was room at the other end of the bar, so Gates went there. He didn't want to interact with Clint Adams if he didn't have to.

"Friend of yours just walked in," Odin said.

Clint looked over at the door and saw Jerry Gates standing just inside, alone.

"Wonder what he wants," Odin said.

"A drink, I'll bet."

"Should I serve him?" Odin asked.

"Of course you should," Clint said. "You're in business to serve drinks, aren't you?"

Gates went past Clint without looking at him and walked to the far end of the bar.

After Odin had served the man a beer he came back to Clint's end of the bar.

"Wonder where the other one is," he said.

"I guess they don't always travel in twos," Clint said.

"He's being real careful not to look at you. Did you notice that?"

"Yes, Jack," Clint said, "I did."

"I'll bet you could scare him off."

"I'll bet I can't."

"How much?"

"Forget it," Clint said. "I'm not going to try."

"Why not?" Odin asked. "You've got your reputation on your side."

"Jack," Clint said, "you wouldn't know this, but the times are few and far between when a reputation like mine is on your side."

Odin frowned, obviously not understanding, but Clint was saved from trying to explain it when the big man had to go off and serve someone. While he was gone Beyla sidled up to Clint and pressed her hip against his.

"How did you like Rose?" she asked.

Clint wasn't quite sure how to answer so he said, "She was fine."

"Just fine? The way she tells it she was great, and so were you."

"You girls are really good friends, aren't you?"

Beyla laughed.

"We'd have to be, to be able to share you, wouldn't we?"

"That's what I meant," Clint said. "I haven't known a lot of women who would willingly share a man."

"Well, you're gonna meet another one tonight. Sif's gonna come to your room—that is, if you don't mind."

"Why would I mind?" he asked, marveling at the closeness of the three women. "After all, I want to be fair, don't I?"

"If you want to be fair," she said, "make sure she comes home tomorrow as satisfied as Rose and I were, hmm?"

Before Clint could reply she went back out onto the floor to work, swishing her hips as she went. She knew he and every other man in the place was watching her.

While he was talking to Beyla he had actually forgotten about Jerry Gates being at the other end of the bar. Now he looked down the length of it and spotted him, still with his nose buried in his beer. Clint was sure that fear had nothing to do with this. He was smart. If they didn't have to deal with each other now, why do it?

"Want another beer?" Odin asked.

"No," Clint said, swirling the last few sips around, "I'll finish this one and get going. I'm going to turn in early tonight."

"You pick out one of my girls yet? Who's the lucky one?"

"Me," Clint said, draining his beer, "because I'm going to sleep. Good night, Jack."

THIRTY-THREE

Al Waxx was angry.

Who did Gates think he was, calling him a moron? Telling him to stay in the room? And telling him not to think?

It only took Waxx a matter of hours to work himself into enough of a state to disobey Gates and leave the room, and the rooming house.

He took a walk around town, hoping to run into Gates, but it didn't happen. He walked all the way to the bridge and thought about walking over it, but decided not to. He didn't know what to expect over there. He'd never been to Mexico, and couldn't speak a word of Spanish.

He finally decided to check the saloon and see if Gates was there. It was not that late, but it was dark, and when Waxx reached the saloon he saw Clint Adams coming out. He remembered what Gates had said before about following the man. He also remembered all the rotten things Gates had said to him.

It was time to prove that he was not only his own boss, but that he could think as good as Jerry Gates any day in the week.

As Clint Adams started walking down the street toward

his hotel, Waxx followed from across the street, where he couldn't be seen.

Clint actually did fall asleep, but not for long. A knock on the door woke him and he was immediately alert. That was because he knew who it was. Just in case, though, he took his gun to the door with him. When he opened the door and saw the redheaded Sif standing outside, he hid the gun behind his back.

"I hope you were expecting me," she said.

You had to be careful, sometimes, with the way you answered a woman's question.

"I didn't want to be presumptuous," he said. "You might not have wanted to come."

"I think we can safely say I'm here because I want to be," she replied. "May I come in?"

"By all means."

He backed away to let her in and took the opportunity to deposit the gun on top of the chest of drawers beside the bed.

She walked to the center of the room, turned and discarded the shawl she'd had around her shoulders. Her cleavage was deep and impressive, and she was taller than the other two girls. Her mass of red hair fell down around her pale, freckled shoulders. She had wide hips and long legs. She was a big girl, all right, and probably not yet twenty-five. If she became any more alluring as she got older no man would be safe from her charms.

"Why are you staring at me?" she asked.

"I think you know," he said. "You're very impressive."

"Impressive? In what way?"

She wanted to be told, so he decided to go ahead and tell her.

"You're not only beautiful, you're tall, incredibly shaped, and you give off a . . . a . . ."

"A what?"

His mind raced as he realized he might have backed himself into a corner.

"An . . . aura."

"Really?" she asked. "What's an aura?"

"It's like an invisible force that comes from a person," he said.

"What's it made of?"

"Well," he said, "in your case . . . it's sex."

"Oooh," she said, shrugging her shoulders, "the other girls didn't tell me that you talk so pretty. Tell me more."

His mind had been occupied by what her shrug had done to her bosom. With an effort he regained control of it.

THIRTY-FOUR

Sif—or Amy—was even more impressive when she was naked.

Her breasts were large and impossibly firm. There were freckles in her cleavage that couldn't be removed with his tongue, as hard as he tried.

"Do you have any freckles down here?" he asked.

"There? No, of course—oh!" she said, as his tongue slithered between her legs while she was still standing.

"Jesus," she said, "my legs . . . are gonna . . . oooh . . ."

The backs of her thighs were against the bed, so she simply fell over onto it, and Clint went with her, his face nestled in her coppery bush, his tongue and lips avidly working on her.

She reached down and grabbed two handfuls of his hair and pulled his face away from her.

"You're gonna kill me," she said.

"Well, I wouldn't want to do that," he said, moving up next to her on the bed.

She reached down and grasped his rigid penis and stroked it.

"God," she said, "you are the prettiest man . . ."

"I'm not pretty."

133

"I'm talking about here," she said, squeezing him. "You have the prettiest one I've ever seen. I just want to eat it up."

"Be my guest," he said.

"Okay."

She slid right down between his legs, didn't stop anywhere along the way, and simply began to lick him up and down. At one point she took the head of his penis in her mouth and thoroughly wet it before releasing it and licking him again. Finally, she took his penis deeper into her mouth, leaving just enough room for her fingers to continue to stroke him. As her head moved up so did her fingers, and then both moved down on him, and soon he was lifting his butt off the bed as he felt the intensity building . . . building . . . and then he felt himself go, and she moaned and held on to him, not allowing one drop to escape. . . .

Later he simply lifted her legs up and slammed his way into her, practically lifting her butt up off the bed. She was so wet there was a huge wet spot—almost a puddle—on the bed. He moved her over to the left to get away from it, but he knew they'd just do it again over there.

"Wait, wait," she said.

"Why?"

"I want . . . something . . ."

"Whatever you want," he said, "you can have."

She pulled her legs free of him, scrambled around onto her hands and knees, and looked at him over her shoulder.

"This way, Clint," she said, "I want you in me this way."

His penis was still wet from her so when he pressed it to her he slid into her easily. She moaned then, a sound like none he'd ever heard from a woman before. It was an animal sound, and suddenly she was slamming herself back against him. He found her tempo, matched it, and then they went on like that for a long time, as if it were

a contest and they wanted to see who could last the long-
est.

It didn't matter who won. . . .

Exhausted, Sif lay crosswise on the bed with her head
on his belly. He reached down and stroked one breast,
keeping the nipple hard.

"The other girls were right," Sif said.

"About what?"

"They said you were special, and you are."

"All of you girls are special," he countered.

"Well, we know that," she said, smiling up at him,
"or else Jack wouldn't have hired us, would he?"

"No, he wouldn't. Tell me something."

"What?"

"Jack doesn't know that the three of you have come
up here to my room, does he?"

"No. Why?"

"Well," Clint said, "he's sort of been hinting that I
should approach one of you."

"Oh? Which one of us is he pushing?"

"He hasn't picked one," Clint said. "He's been urging
me to."

"And which one did you say you were going to pick?"
she asked, rolling over and kissing his stomach.

"I told him it was a tough decision and I was going to
have to think about it."

She rested her cheek against his penis, and it began to
swell beneath her. She rubbed her cheek along it then, as
it stretched bigger and bigger, enjoying the smooth skin
against her face.

"Do you mind if I do something that might help you
decide?" she asked.

He smiled down at her and said, "Any help you could
give me would be greatly appreciated, ma'am."

"Mmmm," she said, rubbing her lips over the smooth
skin on the underside of his penis, "I'll see what I can
do."

THIRTY-FIVE

Al Waxx made his decision. He'd show Gates, and make a move that would make him a big man. Adams was in his room and all the lights were out in the hotel. What better time to bushwhack a man than in the dark, and what better place than his own room?

Waxx loosened his gun in its holster and crossed the street to the hotel.

Sheriff Wade Kantrell was making his final rounds when he saw the man crossing the street to the hotel. He could have been someone returning to his room late, but somehow the lawman didn't think so. Besides, the guy looked familiar to him.

He followed.

Waxx entered the lobby and saw that the clerk was sitting behind the desk, his head listing to one side while he dozed. The register was behind the front desk, and it was open. Waxx only had to walk to the desk, lift it silently from behind the desk to set it on top, and then read the book to find out Clint Adams's room number. That done, he went quietly up the stairs.

• • •

Kantrell entered the lobby, went to the desk, and banged his hand on the top of it. The clerk started awake, almost falling out of his chair.

"Wha—"

"Did a man just come in here?"

"Sheriff? What the—what time is it?"

"Were you asleep all this time, Jesse?" the sheriff demanded.

"Well," the clerk said defensively, "part of the time."

"Damn it!" Kantrell said. That's when he noticed the register on top of the desk, open.

The clerk noticed it at the same time.

"That's not supposed to be there," he said. He grabbed it and put it behind the desk, but not before the sheriff plainly saw Clint Adams's room number.

"Shit!" he said and ran upstairs.

Sif was sliding Clint's cock in and out of her mouth. Clint was gritting his teeth, lifting his hips, holding on to the bedposts in an effort to hold back and make the pleasure last, but the woman's mouth was insistent. She sucked him and enticed him, palmed his testicles carefully, lovingly, until he was on the verge of exploding . . . and suddenly the door to the room burst open, as if kicked.

Clint reacted immediately. He pushed the stunned Sif aside with his left hand and with his right grabbed the gun from the chest of drawers. There was a muzzle flash from the door, then the sound of two shots, one Clint's, and the other someone else's. The man in the door grunted, staggered, dropped his gun, and slid to the floor.

Clint leapt from the bed and ran naked to the door. His penis was still hard and jutting, glistening with Sif's saliva.

In the light from the hall lamp he saw the man lying on the floor, then turned his head and saw the sheriff coming down the hall, gun in hand. He looked Clint in

the eye, pointedly avoiding looking at the naked man anywhere else.

"Saw this jasper out in front and followed him inside,"
he said. "Who got him, you or me?"

"Why don't you take a look," Clint said. "I'll put
some pants on."

Before he could, the door across the way opened and
a middle-aged man and woman peered out. When the
woman saw Clint's erection her eyes widened and she
smiled broadly.

"Emma," the man said, "come inside." He closed the
door with a slam.

"Yeah," the sheriff said, "put on some pants before
you scare somebody else with that thing."

"She didn't look scared to me," Clint said.

"I wasn't talking about her," Kantrell said.

THIRTY-SIX

Clint came back out into the hall with his pants on and closed the door behind him to give Sif some privacy. He was still bare-chested, and he had shoved his gun into his belt.

"Know him?" Clint asked.

The sheriff was crouched over the man, so Clint couldn't see his face until the man straightened up.

"Yeah, and so do you," Kantrell said. "It's Waxx, remember? From the saloon?"

"I remember," Clint said.

"I wonder where his partner is," Kantrell said.

"Probably asleep," Clint said. "Maybe Mr. Waxx here decided he wanted to make a name for himself."

"I'll get some men to move the body," the lawman said.

"Hell," Clint said, "you and I can take it to the lobby. You can have somebody else take it from there."

"Okay," Kantrell said, holstering his gun. "Let's do it."

They lifted the man together, carried him down to the lobby, and laid him out on the sofa there.

"You—you're not gonna leave him there, are you?" the clerk asked, alarmed.

"Just until I can have somebody pick him up," Kantrell said.

"But—but—"

"Calm down," Kantrell said. "Nobody's gonna come looking for a room tonight, anyway."

He looked at Clint and said, "I'll look around outside for his partner. If I don't see him, I'll question him in the morning. Is your, uh, guest all right?"

"She's fine," Clint said, "just a little shook up. Thanks for being there."

"There were two holes in him," Kantrell said. "I'm not sure you even needed me."

"Thanks, anyway."

"In your, uh, position," Kantrell said, "I know I wouldn't have had the time to grab a gun."

"I'm always ready to grab my gun, Sheriff," Clint said. "That's something I have to live with."

"I guess so. Why don't you go back to your room and I'll see you in the morning."

"Good idea. Good night, and thanks again."

As he went up the stairs he could hear the clerk complaining again about the body in the lobby.

"Shut the hell up and go back to sleep, Jesse," he heard Kantrell say.

THIRTY-SEVEN

When Clint got back to the room Sif was sitting up in bed with the sheet around her.

"Are you all right?"

"Oh, I'm fine," she said. "I work in a saloon, remember? I've seen lots of shootings."

Clint walked to the head of the bed and touched the hole in the wall where Al Waxx's bullet went.

"Any this close?" he asked.

She looked at the wall and took a deep breath.

"Not that close, no . . . but then that's not where my head was."

"No," Clint said, "it wasn't."

He walked around the bed, removed the gun from his belt, and stuck it in the holster hanging off the bedpost. That done he removed his pants and got back into bed. Sif immediately snuggled up to him. He left the lamp on the table next to the bed burning for the time being.

"What was that about . . . or shouldn't I ask?"

"I think it was just a case of somebody wanting to make a name for himself."

"By shooting you while you were in bed? What kind of name does that get for a man?"

"More of one than he had. I guess that's enough for some people."

"Did you know him?"

"He was in the Asgard last night with his partner," Clint said. "I think they're waiting for some more men to arrive."

"And then what?"

"And then they'll do what they're going to do, I guess," Clint said. "I can't worry about that, Sif—can I call you Amy? Of all the names you girls have, Sif sounds—well—"

"The silliest? I know. Yes, you can call me Amy. The other girls do."

"Well, Amy, we've had enough excitement for one night. I think we'd better get some sleep."

"But . . . we weren't finished. We were interrupted."

"I didn't think you'd be in the mood—"

"I told you," she said, her hand sliding down his thigh, "I've seen shootings before, but I haven't ever been with a man like you before." Her hand encountered his penis and she stroked it. "Of course, if you're not in the mood . . ."

If he wasn't in the mood, the touch of her hand had changed all that . . . as she was well aware. . . .

THIRTY-EIGHT

Wade Kantrell had to give the man credit. When he confronted Jerry Gates at the boardinghouse where he was staying—and where Al Waxx *had* been staying—the man appeared shocked. Actually, it was the *disgust* that followed that seemed the most genuine.

"That sad, stupid son of a bitch," he swore quietly. "What the hell was he tryin' to do?"

"Make a name for himself, I guess," Kantrell said. "He, uh, never mentioned this to you at all?"

"Oh, sure," Gates said. "I mean, not Adams, exactly, but he always mentioned wanting a name for himself. Now he's dead, the poor, stupid bastard."

"That's the second time you called him stupid," Kantrell pointed out.

"Well, wasn't he? I mean, going after the Gunsmith by himself? What would you call that?"

Kantrell thought a moment, then said, "Well, I guess I'd call that stupid. My point was, did he ever say anything to you about going after Adams?"

"No, not a word."

"Now I've got another question. What are you gonna do about this?"

"What do you mean?"

145

"You know what I mean, Mr. Gates," Kantrell said. "Waxx was a friend of yours."

"Oh, I see where you're going, Sheriff. You think I'll go after Adams because he killed Al."

"The thought had crossed my mind, yes."

"Well, forget it. Didn't we just establish that Waxx was stupid for going after the Gunsmith?"

"Yes, but—"

"Well, I'm not that stupid," Gates said, cutting the sheriff off. "I have no intention of going after Clint Adams."

"That's good to hear, Mr. Gates," Kantrell said. "I wouldn't want any more trouble over this. After all, Waxx made his own decision . . . didn't he?"

"He did," Gates said. "He paid the price, and as far as I'm concerned, that's the end of it."

"It makes me very glad to hear you say that," Kantrell said. "I won't take up any more of your time. I guess you'll be leaving town now?"

"Not necessarily," Gates said, "but I'll let you know when I am."

"You will, uh, be making arrangements to have him buried, won't you?"

"Yes, I will," Gates said. "Is he at the undertaker's?"

"That's where you'll find him, all right."

"I'll take care of it right away."

Kantrell nodded and left the porch of the rooming house where the conversation had been taking place. As the lawman walked away Gates shook his head. What the hell was Waxx thinking? Whatever possessed him to make such a stupid move like going after Clint Adams alone?

And what was the sheriff thinking? Jerry Gates sure as hell had no intention of going after Clint Adams for revenge.

Not alone, anyway.

THIRTY-NINE

Clint was waiting for the sheriff when he got back to his office.

"I made a pot of coffee," Clint said.

"Good."

"I had to scrape it out first. Don't you ever clean it?"

"No need to," the sheriff said. "There's always coffee in it."

Kantrell poured himself a cup and carried it back to his desk with him. He sipped it and then looked at his cup in surprise.

"What is this?"

"It's coffee," Clint said.

Kantrell sipped again.

"That don't taste like any coffee I ever made."

I hope not, Clint thought.

"What's it taste like?"

"It's good," Kantrell said. "As a matter of fact, it's great."

"Thanks."

"And all you did was wash the pot?"

"And put in the right amount of coffee," Clint said.

"You'll have to show me."

"Before I leave town."

"Speaking of leaving town," Kantrell said, "Gates isn't."

"I didn't think he would."

"He says he doesn't intend to come after you."

"Not alone, anyway," Clint said. "It might be different once his friends get here."

"Maybe they'll be too busy looking for Frank Hayes," Kantrell said.

"Maybe."

"Been back to see him?"

"Father Frank? No. Your friend Montoya made it very clear I'm not wanted in his town."

"Why should that stop you?" Kantrell asked.

"Why would I go back?"

"Just to keep him up to date, let him know he's got one less man to worry about."

"You're saying I should go and tell him."

Kantrell looked down at his cup, which was empty, and said, "I'm saying I'm going to have another cup of coffee." He stood up and walked to the pot. "I don't think you'll be having any trouble from Gates. Like you said, at least until his friends get here. You, uh, can still bring, uh, friends up to your room."

"I don't think that would be wise," Clint said. "Not until I know they'd be completely safe."

Kantrell walked back to his desk.

"Which of the girls was it, anyway?" he asked.

Clint smiled.

"Sheriff, I'm too much of a gentleman to say."

He stood up and headed for the door.

"Where are you going?"

"I'm taking your advice," he said. "I'm going to see Father Frank."

"That wasn't advice," Kantrell said, "I was just . . . talking."

"Well," Clint said, "I guess I was just listening."

"One question."

"Yes?" Clint asked, with the door open.

"How come you keep calling him Father Frank?" Kantrell asked. "You know he's not really a priest."

Clint thought a moment, then shrugged and said, "Why not? It's as good a name as any."

Clint stepped outside and looked both ways before stepping into the street and crossing over. Just because Jerry Gates *said* he wasn't going to try anything didn't make it so. For all he knew Waxx coming after him in the night might have been Gates's idea.

Maybe the man was spending time right now trying to come up with a better one.

FORTY

Clint's walk to the church was uneventful in that he
didn't run into Sheriff Montoya. He saw several other
people, but he meant nothing to them, and they meant
nothing to him. Now he just had to worry about the walk
back.

When he reached the church he went inside, hoping to
find Father Frank there. Instead, coming out of one of the
pews, he saw the girl, Carmen. She stopped as he entered
and stared at him. She had black hair and black eyes and
dark skin. She was wearing a peasant blouse which had
been pulled up on her shoulders instead of worn down to
show cleavage. Still, the proud thrust of her breasts was
very much evident, and very much out of place in a
church.

"Hello," he said. "Your name is Carmen, isn't it?"

She didn't answer.

"We met the other day."

Still no answer. For a moment he didn't think she understood him, or spoke English.

"What do you want?" she asked.

"I was looking for Father Frank."

"Why do you want him?"

"Just to talk."

"About what?"

"Is he around, Carmen?"

She didn't answer. The look she was giving him was far from friendly.

"Do you think I'm here to do Father Frank harm?" he asked.

"Are you?"

"No."

"Why should I believe you?"

"Why shouldn't you?" he asked. "I haven't given you any reason to think of me as a liar."

"You are a gringo."

"So is Father Frank."

"Father Frank is a great man," she said. "He is a good man."

"And I'm not?"

She tossed her hair, a movement he found extremely erotic.

"I do not know what kind of man you are."

"Exactly. That's my point. So why do you think so badly of me?"

She hesitated a moment, then said, "I simply want to protect Father Frank."

"Well," Clint said, "he doesn't need to be protected from me. Where is he?"

"He is in his room. I will get him for you."

"Thank you."

She went down the left aisle and through a doorway. He moved to the last pew and sat down. He had not spent very many days throughout his life in church. He found it a quiet place, an eerie place. Maybe that was because he didn't understand religion all that well.

He looked up when he heard a sound and saw Father Frank coming back the way Carmen had gone. She was not with him. He was wearing his priest's robe and collar.

As the man approached him Clint stood up and the

phony priest put his hand out to shake. Clint found the man as disquieting as he found the church.

"I'm glad you came back," Father Frank said.

"I have some news."

"Would you like to go outside? You look very uncomfortable in here."

"Is it that obvious?"

"Yes."

"Then let's go outside."

They went outside and stood in front of the church.

"What's your news?"

"Al Waxx is dead."

"Who killed him?"

"Either the sheriff or me," Clint said. "Maybe both."

"What happened?"

Clint explained how both he and the sheriff came to shoot Waxx.

"That was Al," Father Frank said, shaking his head, "any time he tried to make a decision on his own it was the wrong one."

"What do you think Gates will do?"

"Well, he won't come after you alone, if that's what you're thinking. In fact, he might not come after you at all."

"But I killed his friend."

"Waxx wasn't Gates's friend," Father Frank said. "None of us were friends; we just . . . worked together."

"No loyalty?"

That drew a look from the man dressed as a priest.

"Would I have run out on them with the money if there was?"

"Good point."

"No," Frank said, "what he'll do now is wait for the others to arrive, and then come looking for me."

"And what will you do? Wait for him?"

"I don't know," Father Frank said. "I guess Frank

Hayes would go and meet them head-on, and Frank Hastings would try to avoid them.''

"So I guess it depends on which man you really are, huh?''

"I suppose so," Father Frank said. "The problem is, I don't think I'm sure who I am anymore.''

"I guess you'll just have to figure it out, huh?''

"I guess so. Would you do me a favor?''

"What's that?''

"Would you come to my room with me? I want to show you something.''

Clint looked at the church.

"We can go around the back," Father Frank said. "There's a door that goes directly to my room.''

"All right," Clint said, "let's go.''

FORTY-ONE

As they entered the room Carmen straightened. She had been bent over the bed, making it.

"Carmen," Father Frank said, "I would like to talk to Clint for a little while in here. Could you come back and finish cleaning up later?"

"Of course, Father."

She went to the door to the church and exited that way.

"She actually thinks that the Virgin told her to come to you?"

"Yes."

"Don't you think that's a little . . ." Clint groped for a word he hoped wouldn't be offensive, but he couldn't find one.

"Sick?"

"Well . . ."

"She's very devoted to me," Father Frank said. "And to the church."

"She's very young," Clint said. "Shouldn't some of that devotion be saved for her family?"

"You're probably right," Father Frank said, "but I didn't bring you here to talk about that."

"Okay," Clint said, "why did you bring me here?"

"I'm not sure," Father Frank said. "Maybe to show you this."

He walked to a corner of the room, where a large trunk sat. He opened it, and waited for Clint to come over. When he did he saw a gun and gun belt, a bottle of whiskey, some tobacco, cigars, along with a few other items, none of which seemed so outrageous—there was a vest and a shirt—that they should be hidden.

"What is all that?"

"That," Father Frank said, pointing into the trunk, "is where Frank Hayes is buried—for good, I had hoped."

"So," Clint said, "close the lid and he stays buried."

"That's what I thought," Father Frank said. "But Gates, and the others, they won't let him stay buried. Eventually, they'll find me."

"How?"

The other man shrugged.

"You know how these things work," he said. "They overheard you, they could overhear someone else, as well. It'll happen."

"Not if you stay on this side of the border," Clint said. "Maybe they won't come over here."

"Maybe," Father Frank said, and closed the lid on the trunk.

"Why don't you take all of that stuff out and bury it, or give it away?" Clint asked. "Then maybe Frank Hayes would be gone for good."

Father Frank smiled.

"I think I'm afraid," he said. "What if I get rid of the gun and then Gates and the others find me? Or someone recognizes me?"

"That's something we'd all have to live with if we gave up our gun," Clint said. The "we" he was speaking about was the community—or even fraternity—that he belonged to. The Fraternity of the Gun, it could be called. He and Hayes were both members.

"Have you ever hung up your gun?" Father Frank asked.

"No," Clint said, "never."

"Would you ever?"

"No."

"Why not?"

"Because it's too late for me," Clint said. "I know that."

"Well," Father Frank said, "maybe it's too late for me, too."

"Too late for Frank Hayes?" Clint asked. "Or for Father Frank Hastings?"

"Both," the other man said. "It's about time I admitted that I'm both men. I can't be one or the other."

"Most times," Clint said, "it's hard enough just being one man."

Father Frank nodded.

FORTY-TWO

Carlos Montoya rushed through the door of the house, startling his mother, Consuelo.

"What is wrong with you?" she demanded. "You frightened me half to death."

"Momma, I have news," he said anxiously.

"What news could you have that was so important you had to frighten your mother, eh?"

"I have news of . . . Father Frank."

Now he had her attention. She turned away from the stove and wiped her hands on the apron she wore.

"What news?"

"There are some men looking for him."

"Here?"

"In Valhalla," Carlos said, "across the bridge."

"How do you know this?"

"There has been talk," he said. "I have heard it."

She frowned at him.

"You have crossed the bridge, Carlos?" she demanded. "Your father does not want you boys crossing the bridge—"

"I did not cross, Momma," Carlos said, and she thought he was probably lying, "but I have friends who

159

do, and they have brought back the news. There is a gringo, he is called the Gunsmith.''

"I have heard this name.''

"He has been to see Father Frank. He was talking in the saloon with the bartender, and my friend thinks it was about Father Frank. Then two other men talked with him, and they were looking for a man . . . a man named Frank Hayes.''

"That name I do not know.''

"He is a famous *bandido* and gunman from the United States.''

"What has that to do with Father . . . Frank?''

"Father Frank is Frank Hastings,'' Carlos said, "and the *bandido* is Frank Hayes. Do you see?''

"I see a similarity,'' she said, "but that does not prove that they are the same man.''

"But—''

"It does not matter,'' she said, cutting him off with a wave of her hand. "It does not matter if they truly are the same man, only that these men might think that they are. What would they do, then?''

"Perhaps they would kill him?''

"Perhaps,'' she said. "Carlos, I want you to do something for me . . .''

When Jerry Gates came downstairs from his room he saw the young Mexican man sitting on the sofa in the rooming house living room. The landlady had knocked on his door and told him that someone was there to see him.

"Are you lookin' for me, hombre?'' he asked.

The young man stood up and nervously fingered his hat in his hand.

"*Sí*, señor, if you are the man who is looking for the man Frank Hayes?''

Gates narrowed his eyes and asked, "What do you know about Frank Hayes?''

"I know where he is, señor.''

"Where?"

"Across the border, in the church."

"He's hiding in the church?"

"Señor," Carlos Montoya said, "he is the priest."

"What?"

"*Sí*, señor. He calls himself Father Frank, and says his last name is Hastings."

"And you know this for a fact?"

Now came the lie that Carlos's mother had told him to tell. He hoped that he would not go to hell for telling such a lie.

"*Sí*, señor," he said. "It is he."

FORTY-THREE

The next afternoon two men rode into town, put their horses up at the livery, and then went to the rooming house that Jerry Gates was staying in. The liveryman took their horses in, then walked to the sheriff's office.

"Sheriff, two strangers just left their horses at the livery stable."

"Thanks, Juan," Kantrell said.

The man nodded and left. Kantrell got his hat, strapped on his gun belt, and left the office. He walked over to Clint's hotel. The desk clerk told him that Clint was having lunch at a nearby café he'd found. Before he left he asked the clerk if anyone had checked in recently, and the answer was no.

Kantrell went to the café and found Clint sitting at a back table, working on a huge steak. He walked over and sat down.

"Sheriff," Clint said.

"Two men just rode into town," Kantrell said. "Two strangers."

Clint looked at him.

"Got to be them," he said.

"That's what I was thinking."

"Where did they go?"

"I don't know. They didn't check in at the Midgard."

"The rooming house where Gates is?"

"That, or one of maybe two others. I'll check it out today."

"We'll know if we simply see them walking together," Clint said, "and after what happened to Waxx, they'll be staying together, you can bet on that."

"If they come after you . . ."

"I'm more concerned with them going after Father Frank."

"That's commendable," Kantrell said, "but if Father Frank is Frank Hayes, he can take care of himself. You, on the other hand, better concentrate on taking care of yourself."

"Sheriff," Clint said, "there's nothing else I concentrate more on during the course of a day."

Kantrell stood up.

"I'll let you know what I find out."

"I'd appreciate it."

The sheriff nodded and left. Clint finished his steak, then sat back and worked on finishing the pot of coffee he'd gotten with it.

Father Frank Hastings looked into the trunk, as he had the day before, at the remnants of Frank Hayes. He was surprised to realize that even he thought of himself as "Father Frank."

He reached in and touched the leather of the gun belt, and then the steel of the gun. If he closed his eyes he could feel the gun in his hand. He hadn't held it for months, but this wasn't something you forgot. Not the feel of it, and not how to use it.

But he didn't want to use it. He closed the trunk and turned away from it. He wanted to leave Frank Hayes in that trunk forever, but could he?

Maybe he could, but not until he got rid of what was at the very bottom of the trunk.

• • •

"Whataya mean Waxx is dead?" Sammy Martin asked.

"Just what I said," Gates replied. "Somebody killed him."

"Who?" Dave Barrett asked. "Who killed him?"

"Fella by the name of Clint Adams."

"What?" Martin said.

"The Gunsmith?" Barrett asked.

"That's right."

"Jesus," Barrett said, "how did that happen?"

"It happened because Al was stupid," Gates said. "He went after Adams alone, to make a name for himself, and he got killed for his trouble."

"What are we gonna do about it?" Barrett asked.

"Nothing."

"Whataya mean, nothin'?" Martin asked.

"Do you want to go after Clint Adams?" Gates asked Barrett. The man looked away. "You?" he asked Martin, with the same results. "That's what I thought. I don't want to go up against him, either. Besides, we got other things to do—more important things."

"Like what?" Barrett asked.

That was when he told them about Frank Hayes.

"Frank's here?" Barrett asked.

"Dressed as a priest?" Martin said, shaking his head. It wasn't really a question.

"Not here, exactly," Gates said. "He's across the border."

"They got law there?" Barrett asked.

"A sheriff, I guess," Gates said.

"How did you find out he was here? Or there?" Martin asked.

"Well, first I heard Adams talking about this fella who was handy with a gun and read poetry."

"Frank was always reading them poems, wasn't he?" Martin asked.

"That's right, he was," Gates said. "I questioned Adams, but he was a little evasive."

"You talked to the Gunsmith?" Martin asked.

"Well, sure," Gates said, "I ain't afraid to just talk to the man."

He went on to tell them how a Mexican had come to see him with word about this priest, "Father Frank."

"How do we know this is our Frank?" Martin asked.

"What if we gun down a real priest?" Barrett asked.

"We're not going to gun down anybody without checking it out first," Gates said.

"What about Adams?" Martin asked. "Is he gonna take a hand in this?"

"I don't know," Gates said.

"What do we do if he does?" Barrett asked.

"I don't know that, either," Gates said. "All I know is we're going to have to find out first if this priest really is Frank Hayes. Once we know that, then we can decide what to do."

"So when do we find out?" Barrett asked.

"Now," Gates said, "we find out now."

"How?" Martin asked.

"We just walk over to Mexico," Gates said, "and we take a look."

FORTY-FOUR

"Do not go to the church today," Consuelo told her daughter.

"I must go, Momma," Carmen said.

"No."

"Yes."

"Carmen—"

"Father Frank needs me."

Consuelo grabbed Carmen's arm and held it tightly, so tightly that Carmen cried out in pain.

"Momma—"

"You will not go to the church today!" Consuelo said. She would break her daughter's arm if she had to, to keep her home. She did not want her daughter endangered when the gringos came to kill Father Frank.

"What are you doing, Momma?" Carmen said, still struggling. She had no idea her mother was this strong.

"What is going on here?" Eusebio Montoya demanded, coming out of the bedroom. He was wearing his gun and his badge, ready to go to work. "Why are my wife and my daughter fighting in my house?"

Both women stopped struggling, although Consuelo still had ahold of Carmen's arm. Her grip, however, had lessened, and suddenly Carmen yanked her arm free and ran out the door.

"Carmen! Come back!" Consuelo shouted. She looked at her husband and he saw naked fear on her face, something he had never seen before. "*Ay, Dios mío,*" she said. "You must get her, my husband. You must not let her go near the church!"

Eusebio stared at his frantic wife and asked, "In God's name, what have you done, woman?"

The three men, led by Jerry Gates, strode through town toward the bridge to Santa Maria. Sheriff Kantrell had not even had time to check the rooming house. He watched as the three men walked down the main street to the edge of town, and wondered what to do. Stop them? Why? They were leaving town. Granted, it was only temporary, they were not even taking their horses, but still, they were leaving. However, it was fairly clear where they were going, and Kantrell had no intention of going into Mexico. They already had a lawman over there, let him do his job.

The one thing he could do, however, was tell Clint Adams what was going on. He turned and headed back to the café where Clint was finishing his lunch.

Carmen was as frantic as her mother was when she reached the church. She banged on Father Frank's door until he opened it and then she fell into his arms, panting.

"What is it?" he asked. "What's wrong?"

"I do not know," she said.

He saw that there were bruises on her forearm, seeming to grow darker even as he watched.

"What happened?"

"My mother," Carmen said, "she has gone crazy. She tried to stop me from coming here."

"She did this?" he asked, indicating her arm.

"Yes."

"To keep you from coming here today?"

"Yes," Carmen said. "I do not know what has come over her, unless . . ."

"Unless?"

"*Madre de Dios,*" Carmen said. "What has she done?"

"What?" Clint asked. "When?"

"Just now," Kantrell said. "I saw them going down the street."

"All three of them?"

"Yes."

"They're going for the priest."

"But he's not a priest," Kantrell said.

Clint ignored the remark and stood up.

"Are you coming?"

"To Mexico?" Kantrell asked. "Heck, no."

"Then I was wrong about you," Clint said, and left.

Montoya was on his way to the church when he saw the three men, all gringos.

"Señors," he said, getting in front of them, "you must stop."

Clint hurried over the bridge. As he was doing so he heard a shot. He increased his pace even more and saw the fallen man. As he got nearer he saw that it was Sheriff Montoya, wounded but still alive.

"Señor," Montoya said, when Clint knelt beside him, "you must stop them. They . . . they are going to the church . . . you must . . . you must . . ."

"I have to get you to a doctor," Clint said.

"No," Montoya said, "no doctor . . . my daughter . . . she is with the priest . . . you must help her . . ."

"Montoya," Clint said, "you need a doctor bad."

His wound was in his chest, and it was bleeding badly.

Montoya gripped Clint's arm hard, surprising Clint with his strength, considering his wound.

"You must go!" he commanded, and then collapsed, as if the statement had used every ounce of strength he had left.

"Clint?"

Clint looked over his shoulder and saw Sheriff Wade Kantrell standing there.

"Maybe I wasn't wrong about you," Clint said. "Get him to a doctor, Kantrell."

"What about you?"

"I've got to stop Gates and his men."

"I should go with—"

"No," Clint said, "you have no jurisdiction here, but you can get Montoya to a doctor and maybe save his life."

"All right," Kantrell said, "but after that I'm coming to the church."

"Suit yourself," Clint said, even though he felt that by then it would all be over anyway.

FORTY-FIVE

"You have to get out," Father Frank said to Carmen.

"Why?" she demanded. "What has my mother done?"

"There are some men who want to kill me, Carmen," he said. "I think your mother told them where I am. That's why she didn't want you coming here today. She knew you would be in danger."

"But . . . why would she do that?"

"That's simple," Father Frank said. "She'd rather kill me than have you here with me."

He walked to the corner and opened the trunk. From it he took everything that was Frank Hayes. His vest, his shirt, his pants, his boots . . . and his gun.

"What are you doing?" she asked.

"They are not looking for the man I am," he said, "they are looking for the man I was. I'm going to give them that man."

"I will not leave you," she said stubbornly.

"Then you will stay in here," he said, undressing and then donning the old clothes, "and you will not leave this room. Do you understand?"

"Yes."

"Good."

He had only two things left to do. Strap on the gun,

and take the saddlebags from the bottom of the trunk.

"Hayes!"

He heard the voice and lifted his head.

"Frank Hayes! We know you're in there. Come on out, Frank. It's your old friends come calling."

"Is that them?" she asked.

"Yes."

"They call you . . . Frank Hayes?"

"Yes," he said. "The man I was."

He picked the gun belt up from the bed and strapped it on. It felt as if he had never taken it off.

He took the saddlebags from the trunk and headed for the door.

"Remember what I said," he told her. "Don't come out until I call you."

"Yes," she said, "I will."

She rushed to him, grabbed his hand, and kissed it.

"The Virgin will protect you."

"This ought to be interesting," he said, and went out the door that would take him to the church.

He walked through the church to its front doors, opened them, and stepped outside.

Gates recognized Hayes immediately.

"You shaved your beard, Frank," he said, "but I'd know you anywhere. How are you?"

"I was fine, Jerry, until you showed up."

"Got yourself a nice little setup here?" Gates asked. "Calling yourself Father Frank, I hear."

"I've got the money, Jerry."

"That's good."

"All of it."

Frank Hayes held the saddlebags in his left hand, extended them toward Gates and the others.

"That's real good, Frank," Gates said. "We'll take it from you . . . after we kill you."

"Take the money, Jerry," Hayes said. "Nobody has to die."

"Wrong," Gates said. "You have to die, Frank. You ran out on your partners. That means you have to die."

"Jerry," Hayes said, "Dave, Sammy, I'll take at least one of you with me, maybe even two. Who wants to die?"

"That won't work, Frank," Gates said. "These boys are too pissed off to be bought off by words or money."

"You think so, Jerry?" Hayes said. "Why don't we ask them. What do you say, boys? Want a sure fifty thousand, or do you want to take a chance on dying? What's it going to be?"

FORTY-SIX

When Clint came within view of the church he saw Frank Hayes—and it *was* Hayes, and not "Father Frank"—out in front of the church facing Gates and his two partners. Hayes seemed to be offering the three men a set of saddlebags, probably with the money in them. Clint felt he had two choices—three, actually. He could watch the action from here, simply letting the four men settle their differences. This was, after all, a personal thing among them. On the other hand, the three men *had* shot down the sheriff of Santa Maria only moments ago.

Two, he could run in and possibly instigate an immediate shoot-out.

Three, he could move forward slowly and try to get close enough to be of help if Hayes needed it.

He opted for the third and began to move forward. He never *could* mind his own business.

"Whataya say, boys?" Hayes asked.

"Jerry?" Barrett said. "He's offerin' us the money."

"All of it," Martin said.

"Have you guys forgot he ran out on us?" Gates asked. "We were never the same after he left. He cost us a lot of money."

175

"He's givin' us the money, Jerry!" Barrett said.

"All fifty thousand," Martin threw in.

Gates gave them each a hard look.

"You boys want the money so bad? Go and get it. I want Hayes."

The two men hesitated.

"Go on!" Gates snapped. "Take it and leave. Desert me, the way he deserted all of us."

Barrett looked at Hayes.

"You really givin' us the money, Frank?"

"I don't want it, Dave," Hayes said. "You can have it."

With that he threw the saddlebags toward them. They landed about halfway between them.

"If you try to pick it up," Gates said, "he'll shoot you."

Barrett and Martin exchanged a glance.

"And if he doesn't, I will," Gates added.

"What?" Martin said.

"You just told us—"

"Forget what I told you," Gates said. "I'm not losin' Hayes because you boys are greedy. If you try to take the money and leave I'll kill you. You've got one other choice."

"What's that?" Barrett asked.

"After we kill Hayes," Gates said, "the money's yours. You can split it two ways."

"You mean it?" Barrett asked.

"I do," Gates said. "You have my word."

Barrett and Martin exchanged a glance again, and then Martin said, "That ain't right. We'll stay with you, Jerry. We'll back your play, and then split the money three ways."

"You hear that, Frank?" Gates said. "These are loyal boys. They won't run out on me, like you did."

"Jerry," Hayes said, "you're the most dangerous. I'm going to have to kill you first."

"If you can," Gates said. "Anytime you're ready."

"Just hold it," Clint said, coming up behind them, "right there."

Barrett and Martin stiffened.

"Who's that?" Barrett asked.

"Boys," Gates said, "meet Clint Adams, the Gun-smith."

"Jesus," Barrett said, closing his eyes. He and Martin were thinking the same thing: They should have taken the money and ran when they had the chance.

"What's your part in this, Adams?" Gates asked. "You gonna back-shoot us?"

"There's no need for that," Clint said. "You boys gunned down a lawman."

"A Mexican lawman," Gates said.

"So you'll face Mexican law."

"And a Mexican prison?" Gates asked, laughing. "It won't hold me. I'll get out and I'll come back here and kill Hayes."

"He's right, Clint," Frank Hayes called out. "We're going to have to end it now or he'll keep coming back."

"All right, then," Clint said. "Let's even the odds a little."

He had his gun in his right hand. He stepped forward and relieved Barrett and Martin of their guns, tossing them away.

"Now it's even," he said. "You boys better join me off to the side."

"Jerry—" Barrett said.

"Go on," Gates said. "You're no good to me now."

Both men moved off to the side with Clint.

"Okay, Jerry," Hayes said, "it's just you and me now."

"I always wondered which of us was better," Gates said. "Now I'll find out."

Both men drew. . . .

EPILOGUE

Clint looked down at the grave marker: HERE LIES
FRANK HAYES, GUNNED DOWN BY JERRY GATES. Next to
it was another marker: HERE LIES JERRY GATES, GUNNED
DOWN BY FRANK HAYES. The date on the two markers
was the same.

The graves had been put on the American side of the
border, in Valhalla's graveyard, so more people would see
them.

Clint turned, left the graveyard, and walked back to
town. He stopped first at the Asgard, where he had left
Duke.

Inside he saw Jack Odin behind the bar, and the three
women—Beyla, Sif, and Rovska—standing in front of it.

"Come to say good-bye?" Odin asked.

"That's right, Jack. I'm leaving Valhalla."

"Think you'll ever come back?"

Clint shrugged.

"Who knows?"

"Guess you never did get to choose one of these lovely
ladies, eh?" Odin asked with a smile.

"No," Clint said, exchanging a secret look with all
three, "I guess I didn't, Jack."

He shook hands with the big man.

"Maybe that'll be worth comin' back for, huh?"

"Maybe, Jack," Clint said. "Good luck with building this town back up."

"Thanks."

"Ladies," he said, touching the brim of his hat and leaving.

Outside he found Wade Kantrell waiting for him.

"Headin' out?" Kantrell asked.

"That's right. How's Montoya?"

"He'll make it."

"And Martin and Barrett?"

"In his jail."

"That's good."

"They'll be spending a long time in a Mexican prison."

Clint mounted up.

"Which way you headed?"

"Into Mexico first," Clint said, "and then north."

"Why Mexico?"

"I've got a message to deliver before I leave." He leaned down and shook hands with the man. "Thanks for proving I wasn't wrong about you."

"Thanks for proving it to me," Kantrell said.

Clint turned Duke toward Mexico and rode.

Clint rode over the bridge and to the church. As if they had been watching for him, Father Frank and Carmen came out of the church as he rode up to it.

"Did you visit my grave?" Father Frank asked.

"I visited the grave of a friend of yours," Clint said. "Frank Hayes."

"Ol' Frank is finally dead, huh?" Father Frank asked.

"As far as everyone is concerned, yes." Actually, all that was buried in the grave was Frank Hayes's clothes and his gun. Still, it was the same thing.

"And Sheriff Kantrell?"

"He'll go along with it."

"Good."

"What's going to happen here?" Clint asked.

"Carmen and I have talked it over," Father Frank said. "She's going back to her family."

"That's good. And what are you going to do?"

"Me?" Father Frank said. "I'm going to stay here, Clint, for as long as these people will have me."

Or until the Church finds out that their priest at the Church of Santa Maria is not really a priest, Clint thought. But then, who was going to tell them?

"Adios . . . Father," Clint said.

"*Vaya con Dios*," Father Frank said.

Watch for

APACHE RAID

197th novel in the exciting GUNSMITH series
from Jove

Coming in June!